THE LAST COAL TRIP
TO TENBY

THE LAST COAL TRIP TO TENBY

Rod Humphries

Parthian
The Old Surgery
Napier Street
Cardigan
SA43 1ED

www.parthianbooks.com

First published in 2012
© Rod Humphries 2012
All Rights Reserved

ISBN 978-1-908069-94-8

Editor: Jon Gower
Cover by www.theundercard.co.uk
Typeset by Elaine Sharples
Printed and bound by Gomer Press, Llandysul, Wales

Published with the financial support of the Welsh
Books Council.

British Library Cataloguing in Publication Data

A cataloguing record for this book is available from
the British Library.

For our parents

In memoriam

The victims of April 29th/30th 1941

Grateful thanks to many for ideas, help, fun and friendship.

Especially:

Hywel Gillard

Roland Humphries

And of course, Eric Talbot.

With thanks to:

Jon Gower

Roy Noble OBE &

Penny Thomas

Tenby…

Dinbych-y-Pysgod… The Little Town of the Fishes.

'How do you spell Tenby?

'One bee

Two bee

Three bee

Four bee

Five bee

Six bee

Seven bee

Eight bee

Nine bee

TEN BEE!'

Playground joke, Rhondda, 1930s

'Tenby, second only to Las Vegas for stag parties…'

Newspaper item 2000 (dubious)

'Tenby! Tenby! – Of course it's Tenby; we always go there!'

George 'Hold Forth and Fifth',

Penddawn Coal Trip COMMITTEE man, 1939 [sic].

WE, OF VALLEYS STOCK

FOREWORD BY ROY NOBLE, OBE

We, of Valleys stock or from a Cwm clan, were always on them, those annual pilgrimages; making a dash to the sea, as a commune, with knitted bathing costume, strawberry jam sandwiches and fizzy pop safe in the old army haversack. Well, safe for the first mile anyway, until the first bag was opened and then the habit spread down the aisle to transform the bus into a mobile canteen.

In this book Rod Humphries colourfully takes us back to those long convoys of buses that emptied a South Wales Valley village to fulfil a mission... the trip. It was a good job the Census was not taken on those particular days, otherwise the population of Wales would have been all over the place. Individual chapels, unless they combined together in religious, sea-cleansing fervour and commitment, tended to be sporadic and individual in their arrangements. The Club and Institute were different; it was an all-encompassing, twelve-bus caravan, a totally inclusive quilt, covering all ethnic, religious or national backgrounds. As long as you were a Club member or knew one on the Committee… you were in.

Rod has entirely captured the essence of the famed Valleys trips and I am with him all the way, in mind and bus, because, in truth, my family was always more Club than Chapel. *The Last Coal Trip to Tenby* adds a fuller flavour to my knickerbocker glory of recall. I had my first one of those in Tenby, by the way – it was half a crown, dearer than fish and chips (with bread and butter on the side). There are sub-plots that capture the very essence of Valleys life in that time of long ago and wondrous, tidy summers. We can all relate to the images that massage our memories: the characters, the places, the 'goings on', from the humdrum to the highbrow.

This university of life had two campuses in Penddawn, the Old Curiosity Bookshop and the Club Library. In my village, Brynaman, the university specialised in two areas of advanced study: the Public Hall with its cinema, snooker room and library, and Maldwyn's ice-cream parlour… and snooker room. We were frogmarched as an entire junior school to see special showings of *Treasure Island* and *The Dam Busters*. The class teacher often sent one of us pupils down to the library, in school time, to change his library books, giving the librarian free rein as to choice.

Oh, how I remember the coal being delivered, in a load, and dropped on the road outside the house. As Rod recalls we too, as a family, used a newspaper across the grate to draw the fire. And you knew it was at critical point when the paper started scorching and turned brown.

Secrets were few, relationships were close, toilets were semi-detached, of one-brick thickness, so you could share the morning news with Rhys Price next door. Two doors away lived 'Dai the Gate', whose family had once lived, so I was told, in a toll-gate property. The story is still told in Brynaman of the day Dai picked up his first pastel-shaded toilet paper in 'Jenny Painter's' shop. He'd totally missed new white toilet paper, which was the only colour choice for a year, and leapt from the *Daily Herald*, cut into squares, straight to pastel pink, blue and yellow soft paper. When asked what colour he fancied he was totally thrown and, apparently, responded with, 'Oh, I don't know… something to go with brown!'

This book is a therapeutic exercise in understanding your roots and where they grew. We all had occasions when committees were king, Brylcreem was controlling and a good line of washing marked a woman as a wife of 'grain' and standing. Mrs Jones next door to my grandmother, whose husband Dai cropped our hair and dabbled as a medium, was a woman of tone and sensitivity. She had a great line of washing, graded by items, blankets one end, shirts the other and her bloomers always put inside pillowcases lest the men living in the road catch a glimpse of them.

There are so many hugely enjoyable side-tales from Rod in this book, as we head, eventually to the trip… and Tenby, that we're almost glad to get on board the bus. Incidentally, on the bus, we used to sing 'She'll Be Coming 'Round the Mountain' as well and I can remember the many people who had to travel in the front of the bus because they were easily sick. One of our buses had a permanent forward slope because of so many people 'down the front'… in case.

Tenby, ah, Tenby, a place close to my heart. My paternal grandparents were Tenby folk, so my holiday, every year, was to that magical town. How many times have I jumped off Goskar Rock, roamed the North and South Beaches and stared, incredulously, at those 'posh' people who could afford to eat in the 'Royal Gatehouse Hotel'. Our annual trips were to Porthcawl and Barry, except for one year, when the committee coffers were flush and we went to Aberystwyth. The Trans-Siberian Railway game, played by Eric, Larry and others in this story, tempts me to mention our combined schools' train excursion, by corridor train mind, to the Festival of Britain in London... but I won't.

It has been a pleasure to pen an endorsement to Rod Humphries' endearing screed. I could mention so many things that have turned my mind to memory, to yearning and to appreciating the solid, communal basis of our early formative years. Rod's Boppa was my 'gu... I couldn't say the full Mamgu, so all through life, 'gu she was. There are funerals where I clearly remember the tut-tutting that accompanied the arrival of a relative from Cardiff, who had a passable dark suit and black shoes but, when he sat down, you could clearly see them... brown socks; early married life and the pressures of young men whose minds still yearned for the freedom of the 'drinking bus', but whose bodies succumbed to the narrow rules of in-laws, backed up with the wedding vows. Hints of scandal too, with Eric's 'Dark Lady'. It's all there.

Read on and let the emotions, the recall, the recognition be re-kindled with a reflective smile. It is a warming *cawl*, with ingredients that give tang to the humour, yet with flavours of pathos that serve up sensitivity, making it all supremely real and wholesome. For those of us from the ridges and narrow river valleys of the Klondike and melting pot that was South Wales, it was like this, it really was and didn't it do us a load of good. We are all books in the library of life; some of us novels, some of us pamphlets, but we all have a story to tell. Rod Humphries, wonderfully, reminds us of that.

In this tale of *The Last Coal Trip to Tenby*, Rod is given advice by one of his Old Curiosity Book Shop literary mentors: 'Remember Rod, never read a sequel, and never, ever, see a film of a book you've enjoyed.'

Sound advice on the surface but, thinking about this little masterpiece of a book, I'm not so sure. Enough – like enjoyment – is just a little bit more, so *encore* say I.

Roy Noble

THE LAST COAL TRIP
TO TENBY

The highlight of the year for our sometime-mining community of Penddawn was the annual coal trip to Tenby. And one year was extra, extra special, for me anyway.

I have a very good memory – or, as a relative said of her similar recapitulative powers – I am 'cursed with total recall'.

Some memories are wonderful to bring back to mind, to relive those golden moments now gone...

The try you scored,

The kiss – ah that kiss,

The witty comment,

The... well, you know what I'm getting at.

Of course, there are the other not-quite-so-golden moments which even now have the power to make you...

Scrunch your toes,

Clench your teeth,

And tie your stomach in knots.

Ah, memories...

We are told that what some thought had happened, what we thought had happened and what had really happened are all quite different.

1

As I get older and memories begin to overlap and, yes, dammit, fade, this is an account of a trip I made many years ago. If it appears disjointed and confused, I'm sorry. It is *my* memory, so if it contradicts those who have other recollections about what they think really happened then I apologize in advance: sorry.

Still, for what it's worth here it is, the story of what was to be – although we didn't realise it at the time – The Last Coal Trip to Tenby.

Ours was, I suppose, a typical valleys' community during the Depression. If you want a description of black tips, grim colliery buildings and what have you, read Cordell, Jones or Llewellyn etc... for they will tell you that Dai was killed overground, Ianto underground, and, of course, Blodwen loved the pit owner's son. It was a veritable Eden before the fall... everyone poor but oh soooo happy... need I go on? You've read them.

Yes, we had our rows of terraced houses, we had our nicknames... Jones the Milk, Evans Death, Billy One Eye and Dai, who, when groundsman at the council ground was Dai Clodge, but when he freelanced at the golf club was transformed into David Divot! And, oh yes, Morgan – no job, no distinguishing features, the most bland man in Wales – who was naturally known as Morgan Nicknameless.

But we were also part of a Community... a Community with a capital C. We were a thoroughly close-knit crew. We were in the great valley, but somehow not of it. We didn't stand and shout, 'We are different! We are among you, but not of you.' But we felt it, and believed it; as of course did all

3

the other close-knit crews in the valley who believed in their Communities.

Passing from our little niche in a great valley, our 'patch', our territory, call it what you will, there was no visible boundary between 'Grove' and 'Gateway' or 'Long Meadow' and 'Fulling Mill'. The boundaries were there, as clearly defined as if they were 20-foot walls. We were so deeply ingrained with our own, well, self-importance I suppose you could call it, that attitudes – even specific words, be they English, Welsh or idiomatic – would vary from township to township, from valley to valley. To us places outside our tight circle were as remote as Tibet. Of course we made trips to 'The Big Shops' in Pandy, and not infrequent visits to Ponty's wonderful market or even to Cardiff itself. But everything we wanted was literally on our doorsteps. Corner shops, a Co-op of course and two cinemas – yes, two! Church, chapels, oh yes, plenty of those, cafés (Italian, goes-without-saying) chip shop, a dairy, drapers shop and bakers, a cobblers, our Miners' Institute, very important that, Labour club, Conservative club… (don't ask!), several pubs, an infant and junior school. It was just a short walk from anywhere to butcher, baker or candlestick maker. We rarely had reason to leave our 'Filltir Sgwar', our square mile. Oh, and yes, we had a library, a truly wonderful library; as long as you were an adult and enjoyed TOTAL silence.

I cannot remember a time I couldn't read, and can imagine no greater pleasure than sitting with a good book, not just a good book, any book! In fairness, in later years other pleasures filled my time but now I'm back to my true first love. I had read all the books available in the children's section of our library, most I had read twice, many thrice and several... good old Talbot Baines Reed and his *The Fifth Form at St. Dominic's*, yes, four times I'd read that one and loved it each time! And as for Arthur Ransome...

Their descriptions of lives were as different to those of me and my friends as the lives of the 'People in Other Lands' we suffered in school during our sporadic Geography lessons, which went along the lines of 'Copy out chapter 10, don't disturb me.' And, in desperation, I'd borrow the books of Angela Brazil, or read (and enjoy!) the stories of *Anne of Green Gables*, pretending to the librarian they were for my 'cousin', who was visiting... I don't think she was fooled. Why was I ashamed? They are splendid stories! The problem I had was that as a child I could not be given an 'adult' ticket for another five years... in desperation I'd beg borrow or steal any reading matter. I became quite an expert on canary breeding, embroidery, you name it; I could tell you about it. Couldn't do it, you understand, but golly, I could TELL you about it!

And as for the two 'Edgars', Mr. Rice Burroughs and Mr Wallace, I simply couldn't get enough, despite the nightmares those two worthies inflicted on me!

But there came into our lives a bookshop. Oh yes we had a bookshop; indeed, a very, very special bookshop.

It was a time of incredible hardship. In later years I laughed out loud at Orwell's hero in *Keep the Aspidistra Flying* struggling to keep himself on £2 a week – but still managing to smoke and take his girlfriend out – with a bottle of wine of course. If he'd tried keeping a family of eight on 30 bob a week he'd have had something to bloody well whinge about. The poor sod really suffered.

As for the women… while the men were idle, mothers, wives, sisters and daughters carried out the everyday tasks of keeping the home clean, preparing meals from next to nothing, washing clothes and boiling water – always boiling water – not just the kettle for endless cups of weak, usually sugarless, often milk-less tea, but for every cleaning job imaginable; hand-washing all clothing, 'smalls', shirts and so on – but for sheets, blankets, nappies, everything else, the water coming from a single cold tap.

On washing day patches of the mountain side would be a sea of white because of the sheets hung out to dry on communal washing lines, a sight now lost with the advent of central heating and tumble driers. It was a constant battle for cleanliness, even with the pit closed; dust seemed to cover everyone and everything with a fine filthy layer. I didn't understand or appreciate it at the time, but was told much later, 'The women were little better than slaves'. Yet, strangely enough, it was this dust that they fought against that brought about our one and only holiday of the year.

On the first Monday of every month the coalman's lorry would deliver its black load. It would be dumped, if you were lucky, in the back gully, otherwise, it would be in the front, ready for the dreaded task of transporting the stuff through the spotless house to the shed, cwtch or whatever, for storage in the back garden – and yes, some kept their coal in the bath!

Now, with this delivery you'd get lump and small. The small would be put through a riddle and then used to keep or 'bank' the fire overnight. The stuff that passed through the riddle wasn't much use. Mind you, some people mixed it with soapy water and clay, and after a messy, and time consuming job, made a mixture called 'pele' which burnt in a surprisingly effective way. But having plenty of coal most didn't think it worth the time or effort; after all we did have plenty of coal even if some of it was scavenged from the great tips of waste that hung over us.

Most homes then tended to acquire great heaps of this powdery stuff that was of little use and got dragged through the house on shoes and boots – even when it was wet! Delivery day in the rain was no joke.

Anyway, at the end of the village was a large square windowless concrete shed, about 6-foot-high and 10-foot-square. Built long ago for some long ago forgotten purpose, it was rumoured to have been built as a Zeppelin shelter during the Great War, but as it would barely have held a dozen people I think this unlikely. An iron ladder led to the top and a trap door. Any day would see a stream of people carrying a basin, box or bucket of this dust to put in the bunker.

Apparently 'Bunker Day' had all started at the turn of the century – the last one, not this – in the days before World War I. By working class standards, life in those days wasn't bad. 'Prosperous' may not be the word, but at least there was plenty of work; mines were in full production and everyone worked hard – bloody hard in mostly horrendous conditions – but, there was money. And every last penny was earned.

Then one day a sign appeared on the bunker offering cash for dust! Children, being children, immediately cottoned on to this source of income. Every last ounce of dust – previously disregarded – would be taken to the bunker where it would be collected and a few pennies passed over. This quickly led to arguments about equal distribution and who had taken the most – arguments inevitably settled violently. These things may have tottered on until the novelty wore off and died.

However, some bright spark – no one knew who, but in later years many claimed the idea for their own – suggested that the collection of money raised by the sale of dust should be used towards the coronation celebrations – the second attempt – of Edward VII. This was 1902. A COMMITTEE was set up (oh yes, they loved their COMMITTEES) and a fair price system was agreed upon – to the annoyance of the coalman. Thus monies raised by 'the dust' paid for a coronation party. Horses and carts were provided, food and drink galore, a tent, band and choir and everyone went up into the singing mountain.

It was a day never forgotten by those who were there; a day of entertainment. Finally, there was a dance in the evening for the grown-ups and a mug, penny and bun for the children. All agreed it was a 'never-to-be-forgotten' day, except for Boppa, of course, who called it 'ungodly'. (It was shortly after Eric had left for college…)

Remember. Saturday was a working day, a half day for some, but still a working day. And Sunday, take my word for it, was… well, yes, a day of rest, but not enjoyment for most. So a celebration like that shone out through a working life of what was mostly drudgery for men and women. Yes – there had been 'Mabon's Days' but they were short lived (look it up like I had to). Oh all right, it was the first Monday of every month granted as holiday (unpaid) which actually gave workers a full day free from work without the restrictions of the Sabbath. These days were negotiated by miners' leader William Abraham, known to all and sundry by his bardic name, Mabon, these ran from 1888 to 1898. When they finished there was nothing to break the monotony of the daily grind for the average working class man and woman.

After that first year it was decided to continue dust collecting. Also, collection boxes for odd coins were placed in local shops, pubs and clubs. Businesses contributed and the date of 'the last Saturday in August' agreed on for future celebrations. At first the mountain trips continued – though obviously not during The Great War. It was in 1920 that the idea of a seaside excursion began… and the rest, as they say, is history.

Early trips alternated between Porthcawl and Barry but then, in 1926, the year of the General Strike, Tenby was agreed upon. The trip would go ahead come hell or high water, despite the best efforts of Baldwin, and his floor-crossing lick spittle Churchill; and thank you at least Lord

Reith for your integrity. However, as I said, in 1926, Tenby was agreed upon and despite dreadful hardships, or perhaps because of the hardships, the first trip on buses went there.

So it was throughout the Depression, and despite empty promises from empty-headed royals, the trip went ahead every year without fail. No matter how broke, the widows' mite went into the collecting boxes and that, with the dust money, made it possible.

It was especially good for the village children who otherwise would hardly have left the confines of Penddawn from one year to the next. Our one excursion saw us every Whitsun in best 'bib and tucker' slog up a mighty hill to the site of our holy well. There we would throw pins into the sacred water, with prayer and hymn accompaniment, very nice I'm sure, but very Celtic and anything more pagan you'd have to go a long way to find…

Then it was back to Sunday school for more prayers, hymns and a sermon for good measure.

In fairness we did have a good tea after, but, by golly, we'd earned it! There were no games, and, well, no fun. For us the mountains were our playground, familiar and friendly, a place to play, but somehow this always cast a shadow, for me anyway on the pleasure they could give.

So, roughly every three months, the coalman and his boy would call and clear the bunker. They would spend a busy, filthy hour shovelling the stuff into sacks. The boy, poor sod, was actually *inside* the bunker, shovelling and passing out sacks. Eventually he'd stagger out covered in the stuff from head to foot, even his boots were full, and he'd walk off trailing great clouds of dust. Eric called him 'Panjandrum' – which was beyond me for a few years. The standard joke was told that if the coalman held him by his feet and banged him against the wall he'd get an extra sack and we'd get an extra bob! It was said he went in weighing 7 stone and came out weighing 10! Anyway the coalman would take it away and somehow compress the stuff into nuggets, which he would duly sell on. The money he paid for clearing our bunker would go to the Penddawn Coal Trip Treasurer and this paid for our trip to Tenby.

The Treasurer at that time was Evans the School. No man anywhere was watched more closely, especially after the last treasurer – a deacon of the chapel, a pillar of society – absconded with the cash and the organist's wife – but that's another story for another day. Poor old Evans, if he bought an extra half pint or dared to buy a packet of ten Woodbines instead of his customary five… you can be sure, it was noted.

Yet he was acknowledged as THE MASTER when it

came to the art of dealing with the coalman, possibly the most hated man in the village – next to the Conservative Party Parliamentary Candidate of course. The Trip COMMITTEE would be there to supervise, and every available villager would attend to watch EVANS IN ACTION!

It would start harmlessly enough…

An offer from the coalman…

A look of contempt from Evans…

Another offer…

A comment of mild abuse from Evans…

It would then rapidly deteriorate…

Until everyone was joining in…

'It's a bloody cheat you are… I took ten buckets myself…'

'And I did you crook…'

'You delivered it in the first place…'

'All I had was small and dust…'

The coalman would plead and beg and point pitifully at the number of sacks on his lorry…

Evans, ex-army store man would be mercilessly grinding away…

It made an Eastern bazaar look like early closing day in Esther's wool shop.

Finally a price would be agreed, hands grudgingly shaken, and cash passed over.

The coalman would drive away, angry, very angry – and he was the only man I ever knew with a beard who actually muttered into it.

Meanwhile Evans would stagger off for a much needed, well-earned and deserved pint.

Have you ever carried a large iron bucket of coal dust?

Throughout my life I have a long list of skills never acquired...

I could never get my hoop to roll along nicely beside me...

I could never hit the blasted catty with the doggy...

Whip and top... what a disaster!

In later years, could I get the yo-yo back up with the string?

The hoola hoop...

...and the least said about recording a television programme onto a video or DVD, the better... iPods, mobile phones and I seemed doomed not to get on and I even have a clock radio that is forever telling me it is midnight...

Today in St. Ives' wonderful library, attempts to get me on the internet are doomed...

I am heartily convinced that all these failures are the result of being made to carry buckets of dust at a tender age.

This particular day I was sitting, quietly reading, when

Boppa's penetrating voice came bouncing off the walls into my ears…'Rod… Rod… Rod…'

My stomach knotted, I left whatever cwtch I was hidden in and went to meet my fate.

Her timing was always immaculate…

John Trenchard would be trapped in the vault with Blackbeard…

Or Jim Hawkins, at the mercy of Israel Hands… or on this occasion Toad was just about to escape from prison disguised as a washerwoman (for me was it for the fifth or sixth time?).

I went into the garden. She was standing, arms akimbo, a fearsome sight – to me anyway.

'Nose stuck in a book again!' A statement not a question.

'Another load of rubbish from those useless Rodneys from that useless shop of theirs'

Boppa, my late mam's sister, never had much time for books, apart from the Bible of course, and *Foxe's Book of Martyrs* for a little light reading – *Pilgrim's Progress* was too frivolous: it had a happy ending.

Even more unfortunately my parents had in their wisdom named me 'Rodney'.

Now, a 'Rodney' is, in valley idiom, and as I discovered later in other parts of Britain – you'll have to look it up like

I had to – a term of contempt. A Rodney was and is the lowest of the low, a shiftless idler. The last train from Cardiff, full of the dregs from the city's pubs, was known as the 'Rodneys' Train'. It was, however, a quirk of Penddawn that the word could be used in a kindly way. Coming home one day filthy-dirty, wet-through, after spending hours damming the river, my father said softly, 'Look at the state of you, you old Rodney.' It was said with affection, with love even. But when Boppa used the term… there was no doubting her meaning.

She glared at me. 'Take this to the bunker.'

She meant a great iron bucket full of dust. She disappeared into the house.

I'd known what was coming as soon as she'd called. Bunker Day was almost upon us… the final collection was to be made.

This Monday all of Penddawn were scraping their last ounces to take to the bunker.

Evans the School had developed a twitch and bitten his nails to the quick. He was seen more often than usual at the Penddawn Arms, constantly looking over his shoulder as each and every eye followed his each and every move.

Meanwhile the bucket was still there, laughing at me, full to overflowing. I grasped the handle in both hands and, by straining every muscle sinew and joint, managed to lift it. It was a point of honour to take it from the back, through the house and to the road in one lift. To put it down for a rest would have been an admission of failure. Furthermore, to do so would have left a mark on the immaculate lino, which would have resulted in a short sharp shock in the form of a short sharp right from Boppa. The handle of the laughing bucket therefore reached my chin, while my bare knees brushed against the bottom.

I staggered out to the front pavement – even this was no salvation, the area in front of every terrace was kept as clean, if not cleaner, than any part of the house itself – because it was on public display. You could close your door from prying eyes but the pavement was there for all to see. It was a matter of pride to keep those two square yards as white as driven snow.

Painfully I reached the sanctuary of the road. I now had I suppose a journey of some 200 yards… it was six or seven steps, or staggers.

Bucket down.

Wipe sweat from face.

Rub hands on shorts.

Deep breath.

Bucket up, and so on…

Finally, after a journey at which Lawrence of Arabia would

have quailed, unless he had a camel of course and, besides, camels were in fairly short supply in Penddawn. Finally I collapsed in a heap at the foot of the bunker's ladder. Usually there was a passer-by only too pleased to help, but today – and surprisingly for a collection day – there was no one in sight.

I'd just settled down for a good 'breather' when Eric came from nowhere.

Eric was a former archaeologist and now the co-owner of the Old Curiosity Bookshop, a second-hand bookshop at 84, Heol Y Groes. Larry, his partner, was equally eccentric. Indeed the question was often posed, 'Who was old and which was curious?'

Stories about the pair were legion. How they survived financially was a mystery; they seemed to live under a permanent cloud of debt. Many of us survived on everlasting credit, an eternal unbreaking cycle of things on-the-slate from local shops. Eric and Larry's main supplier of credit was Huw, the long-suffering landlord of the Penddawn Arms. But occasionally even his patience would be stretched. 'They've got enough slate to roof every chapel in Wales,' he'd cry despairingly. On one memorable occasion, when their slate had been stopped, Eric, in a moment of desperation, took a stool from the bar and carried it to 'Uncle's' which was not a relation, but rather the name of the local pawn shop. He got a shilling for the chair, then went back to the pub for a drink. If Huw was surprised at seeing Eric with money, it was nothing like his surprise when 'Uncle' came in later offering to sell him a stool which he assured him would be a perfect match for the ones he already had!

I suppose Dickens could describe their shop... all I can suggest is you watch an episode of *Steptoe and Son*... only in your mind's eye replace the junk in their scrapyard with books... double it... and double it again, then treble it.

Get the picture?

They used the three downstairs rooms of Eric's double-fronted terrace.

There were:

Piles of books,

Boxes of books,

Books on tables,

Books under tables.

Mountains of books!

The books on the stairs leading to Eric's living area would have to be seen to be believed. Shelving – if you can call it that – consisted of planks propped on house bricks which were surprisingly effective, but as the planks and bricks were of all sizes, the shelving was precarious to say the least.

The tables had legs made wobbly by the sheer weight, so heavily laden were they; it seemed as if the overstrained legs would shudder if you so much as coughed near them. There were books hiding under tables, too, as if not wanting to be sold, which, as I later discovered, was often the case.

Each room had, apart from crude shelving which ran along the walls, its own haphazard heaps of books, huge piles of tottering columns in unsafe stacks from floor to ceiling, mountains of books, a Snowdon of books in each corner... a veritable Matterhorn of volumes by each door... a very Everest of books in the middle... a Himalayan range of books reaching from room to room. Then there were the boxes. There were several lovely old Indian tea chests, which no self-respecting grocer's was seen without, various miscellaneous old wooden and cardboard containers and each one overflowing with books. Good old Arthur Mee's encyclopaedias were there in force, three sets, not one of which was complete, and as each set had similar volumes missing, there was not one complete Mee! And of course many, many copies of the many, many histories of The Great War, and more than one copy of Mr. Lloyd George's *War Memoirs*, which were, to say the least, the source of much discussion.

And let us not forget the magazines... great heaps of magazines were scattered hither and thither, a mixture of gardening, cookery, home care, you name it, but you could be awarded a medal if you could find what you wanted without getting hopelessly side-tracked, or totally frustrated.

Books, books, books… everywhere. And, dear readers, remember, there were very few paperbacks available to us in those days, nearly all were hardbacks.

To literally top it all, suspended from the ceiling at head height, hung a great pram which also held books and of which more anon…

Selection of a book could – and often did – result in an almighty CRASH! What today's 'Health and Safety' crowd would make of it, I shudder to think. Between them Eric and Larry knew the location of every book in the place. Some customers would come in just to browse… but many would ask for a specific book. Eric-or-Larry would either go and fetch the copy, or say, 'Sorry, don't have it at the moment, but we can try to get it for you.'

Mind you, I did see the system break down once. Dr. Manson the local GP asked for a copy of Conan Doyle's *Brigadier Gerard*.

'Yes we've got that,' Larry said confidently. He disappeared. A minute later came the call, 'Eric! Where's that bloody book?' Eric joined the hunt. Bumps, bangs and curses ensued from the back room. A flustered Larry then appeared.

'I'm so sorry, but it appears to be out of stock… we can get you a copy.'

'Don't bother,' replied the doctor, 'I'm just going to Cardiff; I'll get one there.'

The doctor nodded, and stepped out to his car.

Just as he was starting to accelerate away Eric exploded from the back room clutching the desired volume.

'Stop! Stop! Here it is!' Eric threw himself in front of the vehicle, which promptly stalled. He passed the book through the window to a white-faced, bewildered-looking doctor.

'That will be thruppence please.'

The coin was passed over. Eric returned beaming to the shop, as pleased as any Olympic gold medallist… totally unaware or uncaring that he had literally risked life and limb for 3d.

No one who really wanted a book would leave empty handed. 'Pay us how and when you can,' seemed to be their motto. Prices were arbitrary, a matter for genial discussion rather than a matter of fact. Prices were lightly pencilled in, so very lightly they could be easily rubbed out or altered, so as not to cause too great a roar of anguish at home when a loaf of bread had been converted into a copy of *Brighton Rock*.

Collectible copies were generally sent off to dealers although many were kept for local clients. Often books were bought to be sold at cost, or even at a loss if it was something really wanted by a friend.

Often someone would pop in with a penny or tuppence to pay off an account.

Or I'd hear one of them say, 'Five shillings? No, that must be a mistake; it's half a crown. Pay it off when you can.' And, generally, most people did. No one was sure if they made any money but they seemed very happy.

But, more importantly, the shop was a meeting place for many in Penddawn. I've described its physical appearance, but the atmosphere... it just cannot be explained, or rather, I can't explain it. We had, as I said, an excellent town library, but in that beating heart of literature from which I was banned the rule of silence was STRICTLY enforced. Our Miners' Institute was very well stocked with not just books, it had a snooker table, cards, dominoes, a great place to put the world to rights. There was our unemployed club, a few cafés, lots of places to sit and yarn. But the shop, THE shop, was, to say the least, a little bit different. It was an all-important bolt hole for many, not least myself.

My first visit to the shop had been a year earlier, some months after it had opened. It had attracted me from the first. A Book Shop!!! A shop, just for BOOKS!!! What more could a boy want?!! I was more than a little wary of going in despite the promise it held. I'd been warned by Boppa from the day it opened in no uncertain terms to, 'Stay well away'. Firstly, I read too much as it was, secondly there was no room in the house for any books, thirdly we could not afford to buy any books… and finally… Eric was a waster… a scoundrel, and yes, a Rodney… He was not to be trusted, he drank… went to Church… and… and… and… was there no end to his depravity… voted Conservative!!!

It was some time after it had opened that I built up the courage to enter. My available reading matter for this particular weekend was sparse even by my standards. As interesting as it looked, I did not really want to read about *Hop Picking in Kent,* and eight readings of *Little Women* was quite enough, thank you very much. Desperation and curiosity drove me to the shop. Boppa had gone to Tonypandy for the morning so there was little chance of being seen, at least by her. I'd be seen well enough by one of her many cronies, and the matter would be reported to her, but I'd deal with that as and when.

Soon after it had opened I'd peered through the windows at what was for me, and many others, a veritable Aladdin's Cave. So I knew what to expect. Remember this was a time when children were very much 'seen and not heard'. Surprisingly, I was not very wary of entering what was, strictly speaking, very much an adult domain. As I hovered outside I was rescued.

Eric came to the door.

'Can I help, cariad?' he said, and I immediately felt he meant it.

'A book, *please*…'

'Come in my boy, come in! Larry! A customer!' This was my introduction to a new world, not just of books, but of people.

I stepped in to this treasure trove hardly able to believe my eyes at such a vision of riches. My total astonishment must have been very apparent.

'What in particular are you interested in…?'

'Wallace… Rice Burroughs… Christie…' were the first names that came to mind.

'Certainly my boy, but certainly…'

He and Larry rushed to and fro for several mad seconds and placed, most carefully, a heap of a dozen books at my feet.

'Pick from these… pick from these…' Treasure indeed. I spent an age over my selection… finally choosing… *Sanders of the River* by Wallace, (Edgar).

Now the question of cost arose. All I had was my Saturday penny, which I shyly offered.

It disappeared from my palm in a flash.

'Excellent! Just what the doctor ordered. We accept this as a deposit for these and all future purchases.'

As thick-skinned as I was, I heard Larry's silent groan of pain at this generous act. Eric, oblivious to Larry's anguish, shuffled through the pile and gave me one further copy, *Strange Poison*, by a writer as yet unknown to me but who would be much loved.

'As worthy as those other greats are, try this my boy.' It was how he was, he would never criticise another's choice, but, rather, make suggestions subtly. In that one gesture he made me a lifelong fan of Lord Peter Wimsey, the best of the best, in my humble opinion, in that genre of story. And somehow so much nicer than today's angst-ridden alcoholic detectives, who you feel are incapable of solving a double parking outside a cinema, let alone catching a serial killer in Glasgow. The niceties of a good old-fashioned, middle-class murder would be totally beyond them. And you know, they are so much more enjoyable.

Larry then appeared, 'While the Penddawn bloody benevolent club is operating you'd better have this.'

'This' was a copy of *Three Men in a Boat*. Two acts of kindness – soon to be followed by a third – which were, directly and indirectly, to have a great effect on my life.

I walked home wrapped in a cocoon of happiness, but every silver lining has a cloud.

All my joy was soon to be snatched from me.

As soon as I walked through the door of our home, Boppa was ready…

'You've been there then.'

A statement, not a question.

'Yes'.

Her network of spies had not let her down. My carefully prepared excuses seemed silly, and were of no avail. Not only had I been to 'THAT SHOP', I had brought back trash; worse, unpaid-for trash. Credit was all well and good, but not from there, and most definitely credit was not for books.

I arrived back at the shop in tears.

It was almost as if I was expected, which, I suppose, looking back, I was.

'Come on in cariad, sit down.' I was sat on one of the few rickety chairs that were available and I told all.

'Right my boy,' said Larry, 'this door will always be open to you, the books are there for you, take what you want, when you want, whenever you want.'

Eric then appeared with a box, yes another one. It was ominously marked 'DANGER'. Once painted bright red, now much faded, it had originally held explosives and somehow made its way to the shop from the local quarry. 'This is yours, young Rodney, your special shop seat, and your own private library. All books in here are yours to read and enjoy. When they are finished, return to the shelves and replace.' It was to hold books about every subject under the sun and, courtesy of Messrs Wells, Verne and others, even beyond that star. As well as the books I would select, there would always be one or more placed there by Eric or Larry, a mixture of fiction and non-fiction ranging from *The Sword in the Stone* (wonderful) to the story of *Scott's Last Journey* (hard to get into but well worth the effort), and such a wonderful and welcome change from those smug *Little* Bloody *Women*.

So the shop became a haven to me where I could sit in splendid solitude, or that wonderful companionable silence that can exist only between true friends. I'd spend hours in their shop, reading, browsing or helping them try to get some sort of order to the multitudes of books. They would pay me handsomely – in books: how else?

They seemed oblivious to the value of money. The 'till' – if you could call it that – was an old wooden box, which had once held bottles of hair oil. They didn't have many customers, at least not in the sense of people who came in and actually bought something. But they had many friends who would call in for either a chat, or just company; the two things I'm sure you understand are not quite the same.

For a start you could have a drink, usually, not always, and not necessarily alcoholic. It was where anyone and everyone were assured of a welcome, where it was possible to sit in a companionable silence with just the hiss of the gas and the tick of the clock, with or without a book, or you could enjoy a general natter about 'cabbages and kings'. But if all days at the shop were special, Saturday afternoons were, well, they were really special; for that was when... drum roll... wait for it... wait for it... THE PENDDAWN LITERARY AND PHILOSOPHICAL SOCIETY would meet.

Its founder members were Eric and Larry, but anyone who came in was automatically a member. The title, although somewhat pompous, was ironic: with Eric and Larry's dislike of formality it was very, very informal but it was indeed very literary.

Refreshments would be provided, usually some bread, cheese, an onion perhaps, or, in season, a cucumber, tomatoes or a lettuce brought from a member's allotment or garden; in winter a great cauldron of cawl, very thin on the lamb, but thick with veg. It would be started on the Monday and added to and spiced up through the week, until it was ready (after much sampling) on the Saturday. And, depending on sales, a flagon or two. Now, the good old OED tells me a flagon was a large bottle for holding wine or other liquors, especially a metal bottle with a screw top, such as was carried by pilgrims. To us a flagon was a thick brown glass bottle with a ceramic stopper, holding two pints of beer, bitter, or possibly Mild or perhaps Dark, depending on personal choice. Members would bring what they could – often two or three chipping in odd spare coppers – to buy a jug of beer from the Penddawn Arms, not that any coppers were spare.

Tea was always readily available, black, no sugar; if you wanted milk you brought your own. A mixture of mugs, tea cups and glasses were used, with jam jars being pressed into service for unexpected visitors.

To say the least they were a most unusual crew.

The conversation would spread out for hours; all subjects under the sun and beyond would be covered:

Books (of course).

Politics.

Religion.

Books.

Politics, politics, politics.

Philosophy.

Books.

Stalin.

Orwell.

Jarrow.

Nationalisation… 'I tell you, we can beat the owners sometimes, the government… never!' Somewhat prophetic… We had reason to remember those words fifty years later…

Picasso.

Moseley.

Hardy.

Jardine.

Shakespeare.

And of course Hitler… Hitler… Hitler…

Comments, sometimes a little sweeping…

'I tell you there hasn't been a great British writer since Dickens!'

This from men who had in many cases had left school at aged 9 or 10… the glorious British Empire…

All this peppered with jokes, black humoured to say the least, anecdotes, puns galore, or a contribution to their long running limerick or Clerihew competition. Great shouts of laughter, raucous voices, voices, voices, raised occasionally, raised in annoyance, but a voice raised in anger, never. The occasional shout of 'Balls! You're talking through your arse,' would be heard. But anger? Never.

The shop often suffered 'power cuts', their euphemism for 'no money for the gas meter!'

Candles would be lit without a comment and the discussion/debate, debate/discussion would carry on as they talked the sun down. Now most of the shop's regulars were used to these periods of darkness and did not mind prowling the shelves by candlelight, albeit with a few usually good natured comments.

'Like being underground again…'

But no one minded.

Hywel and the others would sit happily in the dark chatting about cabbages and kings; or playing that good old standby, 'Trans-Siberian Express', of which more anon. But, after they had gone a thruppence or a sixpence would be found on a shelf or a couple of coppers discreetly left on a table; not always though and certainly never mentioned.

Most of the import of the conversation would pass over me as I sat in my small corner, half listening, reading by the light of a candle in a jam jar, whatever was available, any one of multitude of books selected by me or for me.

Or if I was lucky a copy of the 'Magnet 'and the truly wondrous adventures of 'Greyfriars' and 'St. Jim's' which were as far removed from the lives of myself and schoolmates as you could get.

More talk… more words.

Visitors and/or customers would come in; some to join in the discussion, returning in future weeks as full members. Others would cheerfully – or in a few cases not so cheerfully – serve themselves, holding up a chosen book and dropping money into the 'till' – or, in a few cases, walk straight out, muttering. Comments about 'Worse than the two foot six' would be heard, but no one really gave a damn.

Anyone could help themselves to whatever refreshments were available.

One time stands out for me. During a discussion about *The Merchant of Venice* most agreed that, 'Shylock was an evil bastard who got his just desserts.' But out of the gloom one voice, easily identified by its loud booming tones as that of Yorkshire man Richard Tudack cried, 'I tell you Shylock is one of the most sympathetic characters in literature.' He then proceeded to explain why he thought this was the case. Much above me then what he said, but in later years when I began to read Shakespeare with a little understanding, my sympathies began to lie with Shylock.

Music played a part too. As well as being discussed in the general run of the afternoon, on occasions Sailor would turn up. He was a valuable member of the group, and not just for his literary contribution. Wearing full Royal Navy 'square rig', which he kept immaculate, his gold cap tally proudly bearing the name *H.M.S. Cardiff* ('Led the German Grand Fleet into Scapa my boy') as clean and bright as the day of issue, as were the gold crossed flags of the signal branch he sported. ('Bunting tosser my boy, only job worth doing in the Navy.') The only things faded about his uniform were his medal ribbons. ('Not important, not important… long time ago, long time ago, memories fading like my ribbons…')

Sailor roamed from valley to valley, staying where he could, his few possessions in a great wooden trolley which he pulled from place to place in the manner of a rickshaw trundling along. His pride and joy and sole means of support was a beautiful old wind up gramophone with a huge shiny brass horn which was out of date even then; and a collection of records, his 78s. On his travels he would swap, beg, borrow or steal, no, not steal, *acquire* new records and earn a few coppers by playing on street corners, or even at peoples' houses; his selection of hymns and arias often being in demand on a Sunday evening. Arriving at the shop he would make a dash for the food and drink (not necessarily in that order) and then play requests so the shop was filled with a mixture of choirs, jazz, opera, Gilbert and Sullivan, orchestras and the big bands and popular songs of the day. And one unforgettable time, Beethoven's Ninth played on what must have been twenty records, a most interesting experience, but one – in those pre-LP/CD days – we enjoyed thoroughly, despite the intervals of record turning and winding, it was all we knew. Sailor had earned my eternal gratitude when once, from the depths of a kitbag, he presented me with a cap tally ribbon embossed proudly in gold block letters with the name: *H.M.S. RODNEY.* 'A great ship,' he told me, 'named after a great man.' I kept this treasure in the shop; to have taken it home would have undoubtedly resulted in its destruction at the hands of Boppa. 'You don't know where it's been!' Somewhere along the way, at a nod from Eric, he would slip in my favourite piece, 'The Laughing Policeman', which caused a mixture of curses and cries of approval. The playing of this anthem was the sign for me to leave.

And of course there was trawling. Once a week one or other of them would vanish with several great canvas holdalls which had been handmade by Sailor, each big enough to hold a small library plus a leather satchel or two held together by string and faith, and whatever running repairs Sailor could manage. He'd re-appear a day later laden with books. This was trawling – going from town to town, market-to-market seeking new stock. The next day the other partner would vanish with a slightly emptier satchel delivering orders far and wide, door to door, and bar to bar.

About every six weeks Eric and Larry would disappear for a 'double' or a 'Trawl Fawr.' They would return two, three or even four days later with bags, boxes and bundles of books held together with string, or on one memorable occasions stowed in the aforementioned pram. And, I mean A PRAM, not one of those fiddling little things that are to be seen today, but a great juggernaut of a vehicle. As they returned from one trip to the Aberdare Valley, they'd picked up this great thing and returned to Penddawn on foot, with it full of books and bottles. They had returned late at night, and as they rattled up the road you could see and almost hear the swish of the curtains and sense the glares of disapproval at the sight of grown men slightly worse for wear. They hushed the 'babies' in the pram with a mixture of 'Ar Hyd Y Nos', a chorus of 'Trelawney', and 'Shut up you little bugger or you'll get a tater'. This did not go down well with some, only some, of the good folk of Penddawn.

I knew after a trawl there'd be work for me the next day, sorting into piles the fresh stock:

Shop pile – for sale in shop.

Larry's pile – his private library.

Eric's pile – his private library.

There was usually something for me too.

I've known the shop pile consist of two books, and seen Larry staggering off to his digs covered in books.

He had so many books in his room at the digs that he had to undress outside and walk in backwards to get to his bed without knocking over any precarious stacks.

He was once asked if he'd ever been married or had a woman in his life? 'A wife? No. Women? A few,' he'd replied. 'But, it was bonnets or books you see.'

On occasions a smartly dressed woman would step off the train from Cardiff and stride purposefully to the shop. Her appearance through the front door would be followed by the rapid disappearance of Eric from the back straight into the strictly 'Men Only' bar of the Penddawn Arms. I'd hear Larry saying 'Haven't seen him for days my dear. No, I don't know when he'll be back.' She'd hang around for a while and then slink back to the station – dejected in this instance, while Eric could be observed gazing, white-faced from the window of the pub. Although on one occasion, which I shall recount later, she had a memorable victory. He called her his Dark Lady. 'Rod, whenever you see her tell me,' and I, rightly, or wrongly, obeyed.

'Hello Rod, want a hand?'

'Please.'

He climbed the ladder effortlessly, arms made strong, not by hewing coal, but by hauling books.

He came back down, blinking the dust from his eyes.

'A full bunker Rod, looking forward to the trip.'

He paused… 'Sorry, cariad.'

And you knew he really meant it,

'Just, wait a minute here, bach.' He strolled off to the 'Branch Office' of the Bookshop… actually the Penddawn Arms! Boppa had – grudgingly – promised to take me on the coal trip. Da had always gone but now he was in Slough scrounging what work he could, sending back to us whatever he could whenever he could. Boppa had said clearly that I had to be on BEST BEHAVIOUR, or else, NO TRIP. She didn't want to go and would have been glad of any excuse. I was the most perfectly behaved child in Penddawn, nay the world!

Then came St. John of God's Day. I was in the bookshop; Larry came in with a candle, placed it in a holder and called Eric who came in with a box of matches. 'Oh dear,' I thought, 'another power cut.' But this day was different. Eric lit the candle, and they shook hands and raised battered old enamel mugs filled with beer in a toast.

'Friendship.'

'Friendship.'

They clinked mugs and drunk deeply.

'Rod,' said Larry, 'we opened two years ago today.'

'Today,' continued Eric, 'March 8th, is St John of God's Day. He is the patron saint of booksellers. We celebrate our anniversary and his memory each year in this way.' He ducked behind a pile of books for a second and popped up with a candle and his box of matches.

'Here,' he said, 'light this tonight in memory of St John, think of him, and all booksellers.'

Earlier that day, when I'd been lighting the living room fire, I'd put a sheet of newspaper over the flames to help it draw. Now, it was a sheet the meat had been wrapped in… it was clean, but it was also… THE NEWS OF THE WORLD!!! Boppa would have preferred to have Satan in the house!

I was deep in juicy scandal – I couldn't understand it but knew it was 'naughty!'

I smelled burning; a great scorch mark appeared which rapidly became a flame. I grabbed the burning paper, scrunched it, and threw it into the now roaring fire. Boppa was there, sniffing…'You be careful my boy, or NO TRIP.'

It was an omen.

39

I had no light in my bedroom, we didn't have electricity, our sole gas light was downstairs, candles were banned, both from the point of view of safety and to stop me 'straining my eyes' by reading. But that night, as instructed, I solemnly lit my candle. I was nervous, I shook, hot wax hit my hand, and I jumped and dropped the damn thing. It rolled off the counterpane on to my rug. It was a typical rag mat, a piece of sacking with scraps of material threaded through – very effective in winter – also, very flammable, it flared up. I quickly extinguished it by rapid application of liquid from a handy receptacle… the smell was appalling.

'You had your chance, clean up, NO TRIP.'

I suppose when you are ten heartbreak can mean a number of things, but at that… I was inconsolable.

I couldn't blame Boppa; it was my own fault, if the bedding had caught alight…

That had been five months previously; I hadn't begged or pleaded as it would have been of no use.

Larry and Eric were very sympathetic I know they felt very guilty. They never went on the trip themselves, but sat in the garden of the branch office with a crate of flagons and 'kept an eye on the village' as they put it. You could leave your doors open of course… mainly because no one had anything to steal. The poorest man in the district was Jones the Thief.

As the time for the trip came closer and talk about it – become more intense, that did hurt. The first Monday in August was always 'Coal Trip Decision Night.' I'd gone with my mates – and Boppa's grudging permission – for the announcement.

The COMMITTEE meeting behind closed doors in the private lounge of the Penddawn Arms would decide, not just our destination, but of equal, possibly greater importance, how much spending money would be available.

Men would wait outside the lounge and crowd the bar, women and children gather in the street. You almost expected to see white smoke billow from the chimney of the 'Pen' when the decision was reached.

Finally George 'Hold Forth and Fifth' would appear from the lounge to make the announcement.

'Tenby! Of course it's Tenby, we always go there.'

The dramatic effect was lost somewhat in that he spoke in such a quiet voice that only a few could hear, but then a rumble resonated through the night…

'… Tenby… Tenby… Tenby…'

'Yes, we know, but how bloody much?'

And as the figure was imparted to the listeners, calculations would rapidly be made to the accompaniment of sighs, smiles and muttered asides.

I was told later that at the actual discussion the odd voice would dare to mutter, 'Porthcawl' or 'Barry' and to be quite fair these suggestions would be given due consideration, indeed enough consideration to refill a glass or two perhaps.

I felt very empty when the news reached us, I'd have my share of 'goodies', sweets and the like, but it wouldn't be the same as going.

Mind you, even today when I see or even more remarkably hear the word COMMITTEE it's always in capitals. COMMITTEE men – yes men only – in the valleys saw themselves as very important and didn't let anyone forget it. In all fairness they did the jobs no one else wanted. They were elected, but at the same time in a minority, if that makes sense. And mark my words; a place on the COMMITTEE was for life! They had power and didn't they just love it.

My eyes opened.

Eric had re-appeared.

'We, and by we, I mean you, Larry and I are going to Tenby.

'We shall be trawling, we have never trawled Tenby, you will accompany us.'

'But Boppa…'

'Leave Boppa to us, well, to me.'

Well I left Boppa to them – or Eric, it was only later I

found out what was said, but I'm sorry – yes that's another story.

Tuesday's meals were banged on the table with more force than was strictly necessary.

'I suppose you can go on that trip with those Rodneys. Three Rodneys together. What your father will say when he finds out – AND he will find out – I have written to him… he can still stop you. Why you can't stay here like a Christian…'

I didn't care… her words rolled over me…

I was going to Tenby, with Eric and Larry, and we were going trawling.

AN INTERLUDE

Saturday August 26

The sun shone hot that Saturday morning – I'm sure it did – it was always fine for the coal trip. I suppose if I'm honest, it would have to be like Dylan's memories of Christmas…'Did it rain for six hours when I was five, or five hours when I was six?' Sorry Dylan.

There'd been talk of postponing, – or even – heaven forbid – actually cancelling it. Apparently some sort of trouble was taking place in Europe again; it didn't mean a lot to a child. I knew we'd go; we always went. If necessary, we'd take our gas masks. A group of local youths had sent a telegram to Germany:

'Dear Adolf, Don't start anything; it's the Coal Trip.'

I often wonder if he received it – he was certainly to have his revenge later. Bastard.

Larry and Eric came to the house to collect me. Boppa was waiting.

'Make sure you look after him, if he goes in the sea and gets his hair wet… or… or… or… if anything happens to that child, I'll not be responsible for his father's actions – or more important, MINE!!! UNDERSTAND?'

To Boppa, going outdoors with wet hair was seen as a sin only second to running naked through the village on a Sunday, bursting into the chapel at the height of the sermon and shouting obscenities at the congregation. I kid you not.

But I must add in fairness to Boppa, going out with wet hair was to her and others of her generation a definite health hazard and a certain ticket for a ride in the fever cart to the terror of the isolation hospital… just as surely as reading in bed was '… bad for the eyes'.

Eric, always the gentleman, raised his beret.

'I assure you, Bron…'

'Don't you Bron me!'

'I assure you… Miss Butler… that no harm…'

She cut him off short – 'You'd better. Now, be off with the three of you.'

As I turned she caught my hand. 'Here,' she said, 'take this.' *This* was a quick, dry kiss on the forehead and also, a silver thruppence pressed in my hand.

Everyone was congregating by the bunker, the air buzzing with excitement. Remember, this was the one holiday of the year for most of us. The ONLY time a lot of people left, not only the valley, but Penddawn. A few surprised glances were cast at Eric and Larry. They gave their dust so they were fully entitled to go. They'd never been on the trip before; they generally stay as I said, to keep an eye on the place.'

Mind you, some of the looks were quite hostile... sly stares, dark glances, disapproval, whispers.

'...sold books at poor Hywel's funeral...'

'...down the house before the ink was dry on the death certificate...'

I squirmed, though the two singled out for attention seemed oblivious to any ill-feeling.

It wasn't really quite as bad as it sounds, well, yes, it was actually... and if they knew the full story it was even worse!

I must now interrupt our preparations for the trip to bring you a story... it can be another tale for another day and you can move to catch a bus to Tenby, but, for the story of:-

The Weeping Widow

The Bibliophile and his Books

Or, the title I prefer:

IT'S WHAT HE
WOULD HAVE WANTED

Eric and Larry had a much-valued customer called Hywel May. And, Hywel like all, well, nearly all of their customers, was a friend and – in his case – a much loved friend of both.

Hywel, like many before him, had left the valley after the riot and long bitter strike of 1910/1911 and gone to seek his fortune overseas. He was one of the lucky few... he had actually succeeded. No one knew where his money came from.

Silver in Mexico?

Gold in Canada?

Oil in America?

Piracy and banditry were among many other suggestions. Whatever, he returned in the early 1930s as a wealthy man, with a healthy bronze tan and a fine line in highly coloured shirts.

He caused a few ripples in Penddawn not least when he bought his parents' old terraced house, which was unusual.

Most people rented, but fair enough he was, 'Always a bit sentimental, old Hywel.' But then he bought the adjoining house, hired builders and 'knocked through' to make one, large-by-valley-standards large home. That was seen as an unnecessary sign of his wealth, a case of showing off: a single man, what did he need all that space for? But a builder he employed told of even stranger things... of rooms lined with shelves from floor to ceiling... 'And, and... he's got two, yes, two I tell you, two toilets – both indoors! I mean, he's only got one arse!' Even stranger, he cooked in the garden! The workmen built a strange brick structure which he said was a 'braaivleis', what we would call a barbeque today. To us a 'barberqueue' was a line of men waiting for a short back and sides. On occasions he would invite friends around for strange spicy sausages and odd bits of meat fetched especially for him by Larry or Eric from Cardiff or Swansea markets on one of their trawling trips. Cooked in clouds of smoke it was either burnt or raw or both, served up on great hunks of Letty's finest bread with mountains of Mr Heinz's baked beans which he called 'boontjies' but there was always plenty of beer, so who cared? Although I did overhear one comment: 'I don't know about you boys, but I cook in the house and do my business in the garden, but Hywel, bless him, cooks in the garden and does his business in the house!' (He didn't say 'business'.)

A second, minor stir came when he became a regular visitor at Eric and Larry's bookshop. You see, he too had a love of books – a passion even. A van had arrived from London laden with boxes of books which he, Eric and Larry arranged meticulously on his mighty shelves. He read avidly and widely, but his main love was collecting and developing his own private library. Any 17th, 18th, but mainly 19th century novels, especially first editions, especially Dickens. Eric or Larry often went to London to pick up copies for him – 'I'm not trusting that particular volume to His Majesty's Post Office, thank you.' On a number of occasions one of the two would be sent to bid at an auction for a sought after Pepys, Swift, Bunyan or of course Dickens.

Then came the ripple of ripples, the triple ripple, the SHOCK OF SHOCKS!

At the age of 65… he married. This triggered more than the normal number of raised eyebrows…

She was not from Penddawn…

She was not from the Valley…

She was not even Welsh… pause… she was English!

She went to church… and… and… my God… she was 40 years his junior!!

He'd met her on a book-buying trip to Cornwall… he should have gone to Cambridge! But as he later recounted: 'Got drunk in Bristol, paid a guard to put me on the St. Ives train and the silly so-and-so sent me to Cornwall!' She'd been a chambermaid in the hotel he'd stayed at… it was love at first sight… etc., etc. 'First sight of his wallet,' some cynics said. Regardless, April May came into our lives. Whatever the circumstances they seemed very happy, the gossip gradually died down, especially when it became obvious that she wasn't 'with child'. However, the happiness soon suffered an early setback.

One day some months after their wedding he came into the shop… obviously upset, and even more breathless than usual. 'Larry, Eric, Rod,' he said.

'She… I mean my dear April of course…' He paused; he could hardly get the words out… 'She can't abide books…' There was a long, long silence. I suppose it was like Midas's wife saying she wasn't too keen on gold. He managed to continue, 'She asked me the price of my latest buy – George Eliot, you remember? Lovely edition of *Mill on the Floss*…' We nodded. 'We have no secrets – I told her the cost… My God – I thought she'd have a heart attack, boys.

'How much?' she asked, then.

'HOW MUCH?' she screamed, then.

'HOW MUCH?' she absobloodylutely yelled… 'But

you've already got books – shelves full of books…' and then she stormed out. I had to put the kettle on and sit down to recover. I'm glad I didn't tell her the true price, by God. She was back in twenty minutes. 'I've just been down to the library,' she raved, 'I've checked and they've got that *Pill on the Moss* there.' He paled. And then she added, 'And other books by that bloke George Eliot they've got lovely shiny covers and are much newer and nicer than that tatty old thing you've got. And what's more, when you've read it, you can take it back and get another one!'

We sat in silence.

'I know I was an old fool marrying her. We are not unhappy; she just can't bear to see me with – in falsetto "Your nose stuck in a book all day".'

We sat in more silence.

'She keeps telling me to dig the garden over, get an allotment, paint a door, wall-paper a room… she calls it doing-something-useful.'

We sat in even more silence.

'I mean boys, I've got Morgan in three times a week to do that – not the brightest of men, but by God he's good with his hands and he's got the greenest fingers I've ever known. I used a bloody spade for the last time on the veldt five years ago; I'm not picking one up now.'

We sat in silence.

'Well, my friends, I'm just going to my solicitor… No…' he said, seeing our shocked faces, '…not a divorce – I'm changing my will. She gets the house and money,' and then he paused, 'but you get the books.'

Now, Larry and Eric were kind men, very kind men, but, books… I'm afraid at this news their faces visibly lit up… you could see each one deciding which they would keep and which they could sell… I'd seen the first edition of *Treasure Island* Hywel had and I'd seen the film *Captains Courageous* and knew what Freddie 'Harvey' Bartholomew thought of it.

'I trust it will not be for a long, long time, Hywel, old friend,' said Eric, meaning it. 'I'm not a bloody fool,' said Hywel. 'At least, I'm not a total bloody fool anyway but if the books go to her, they'll be on the dump and gone forever. You'll see they go to good homes. Anyway, I have promises to keep on this frosty day. I'll see you all again.'

Hywel, dear Hywel. Chapel from the top of his hat to the sole of his boots. And, unusually for those times, a staunch Welsh Nationalist, a member of the embryonic Plaid Cymru, and as devout a republican as Eric was a monarchist. They were, to say the least, a highly unlikely group of friends. Many were the times they 'talked the sun down'.

We sat in silence.

Eventually, after a cold damp winter, poor old Hywel became first housebound and then bedridden, laid low by bronchitis and of course, by the curse of all miners, the dust, the fine powder of the diamond mines, pure carbon, even more deadly than that of the coal pits. April looked after him well, too well; all visitors were strictly limited to a few minutes, and as for books…

'If he'd spent more time in the garden instead of stuck indoors with his nose in a book he wouldn't be stuck in bed today,' she said.

Most people gave up calling, although on one occasion April invited the vicar. He asked Hywel if he was prepared to meet his maker, whereupon he received a copy of Gibbon's *Decline and Fall* – Volume Two – between the eyes and a cry of, 'Clear off, you bloody old ghoul!' The good reverend's black eyes were the talk of Penddawn for quite a while.

Eric, Larry and I stuck at it. Eric would keep April talking at the front door; Larry would fetch a ladder and place it at Hywel's window which I'd scurry up with a trawling bag full of, what was for Hywel, lifeblood.

Finally, he succumbed. The news came to us via a friendly neighbour.

I'm sure you've seen the scene in a cartoon where a character leaps from a chair and leaves a cup and/or cigarette suspended in mid-air, or perhaps Laurel and Hardy trying to get through a door at the same time... it was like that!

'Follow on Rod,' came the distant cry. 'We'll need every hand.'

They arrived at the house... I kept discreetly out of sight.

April answered their knock.

'The vultures have arrived,' she sobbed.

Larry flushed. Eric, always the gentleman, said, 'Madam, your husband, as well as being a customer of ours, was first and foremost a very, very special friend whose company we enjoyed. We offer you our deepest sympathy and if we can help in any way you only have to ask. Now, may we pay our last respects?'

She sniffed, and nodded.

The two went in, re-appearing in ten minutes.

'A good man,' from Larry.

'I agree.'

A pause.

'What a bloody library.'

Then, the front door re-opened. 'Right, you vultures,' from a now clothed-in-black and red-eyed April. 'I have to see my solicitor. Any books left when I return are going straight to the dump. I'll soon have this house – 'House not home,' as Larry later commented – 'I'll soon have this house looking like a proper Christian place... not like' – a sneer

– 'not like some tatty second-hand bookshop… or' – another sneer – 'a Miners' Institute…'

She stormed away.

She had never adapted to valley life.

'Right,' said Larry, 'Let's get cracking. We'll need trawling bags and boxes, as many bloody boxes as we can lay our hands on.' He hesitated, 'Poor bastard isn't even cold; perhaps we are vultures?'

'Rubbish!' quickly from Eric. 'It's what he would have wanted.'

We began the mammoth task of transferring a lifetime's collection to the shop – a distance of some quarter of a mile. Care was vital, copies were old and many were fragile and we desperately needed time. Even Eric's normal optimism seemed to suffer a breakdown.

Just then, the man who made the biggest boxes in Penddawn arrived… Harry 'Box-"em-in" Evans… yes, he was our local undertaker.

'Hello boys, sorry about Hywel, good bloke, had his box ready for some time; he ordered it special, solid oak, carved with a lovely Welsh dragon, a leek and a flower, a protea or something he called it.'

I suppose, dear reader, you can see what will happen? Larry and Eric had been exchanging looks; Bill owed them a favour. Not very long ago he'd bought a brand new second-hand motorised hearse; it was the talk of the town. Many of the older folk were appalled… railed against it. Horses were good enough for my father, and his father before him…

'I'm not risking my life having my body taken in that…'

They all conveniently forgot that the cemetery was at the top of a damn great hill which had on occasion necessitated grieving mourners putting shoulders to wheels for the last hundred yards. It wasn't half a bugger on a frosty day I can tell you.

Bill was worried as he'd sunk his savings into the purchase. If no one trusted his services he'd 'go under'… then, quite luckily, a local dignitary and former rugby star who was family died. Bill was saved; he and his new hearse were booked.

But, then came disaster. As he was driving to the deceased's house to take him firstly to the chapel, then to the cemetery, it broke down… outside the bookshop. Bill was distraught… 'Over 150 mourners!' he wept… 'All that ham!'… He could see his head on a pole. Funerals were important in the valley. Larry was the man of the moment. He whipped up the bonnet, fiddled for a couple of minutes… 'There you go,' he said, 'Sweet as a nut, courtesy of His Late Majesty's Armed Forces.' Bill was effusive… 'I owe you one boys; I won't forget this – ever!' He was about to regret that particular promise.

'Bill… oh Bill… your hearse… and that box… the long one…'

The poor man went quite pale…

'Quickly now, let's get cracking…' He had no chance… 'After all,' said Eric… 'it's what he would have wanted, you know.'

And so, Hywel's library was transferred to The Old Curiosity Bookshop in his coffin. As tall as Hywel was, it still took a good few trips but finally the deed was done. It was all very discreet you understand. As we were about to commence the task of sorting through the heaps Eric disappeared for a moment. He returned from his living quarters with one of the prides of his collection – Dickens' *A Christmas Carol* in a very early edition, possibly the first, the one with the poison cover (arsenic was used for the colour if you are really interested). Hywel had always envied it, but Eric had been adamant. 'Sorry, mate, present from someone special – sentimental and all that.' And Hywel, although he obviously coveted it and I know offered a lot of money for it, never pursued the matter, but handled it with love every Christmas Eve when the four of us took turns to read from it.

Bill and Larry were just preparing to re-load the empty

coffin back into the hearse. 'Hang on,' said Eric. He opened the book and began to read aloud the first few paragraphs... 'Marley was dead...' He finished reading; he and Hywel had been good friends. He closed the book, looked at the lidless coffin and hesitated. Our eyes met. 'Rod,' he said... 'he couldn't have this book when he was alive...'

I gulped and swallowed, my eyes filled...

'And...' he continued, '... I'm damn sure he's not going to have it now he's dead!'

Never one for sentiment was our Eric.

There was a good turnout at the cemetery. Apart from April he had no known surviving family but locals were there in force to say their farewells. Also in attendance were dealers and collectors from all over the country, to both pay last respects, and to see what was on offer.

As the vicar droned on, Eric and Larry were furtively moving among the mourners, showing lists, making notes, pocketing money. Deals and orders were later completed in the bar of the Penddawn Arms. Both were heard to say at frequent intervals, 'It's what he would have wanted.' They were very unpopular in the eyes of many for some time after, funerals, as I said, being very important in the valley. References were made to "traders in the Temple".

I didn't go to the funeral... I stayed home and gloated over my first edition of *Treasure Island*. You know, 'I'm sure it's what he would have wanted.'

Meanwhile, back at the bunker... there was a peal of laughter... Everyone looked at someone who seemed to be enjoying herself...

It was the weeping widow herself, looking stunningly attractive – if not the best dressed, the most expensively dressed lady on the trip. Both her arms were wrapped firmly around Morgan Greenfingers – and both of his were wrapped firmly around her. He'd never read a book in his life but carried away all the prizes at the annual allotment competition.

And as Larry said, in a very loud aside, 'Hywel always said he was good with his hands.'

MEANWHILE, BACK AT THE BUNKER...

Sunday best was certainly the order of the day. Everyone made a supreme effort. The previous day I'd seen next door's children playing in their nightwear – no, not pyjamas or nighties but old, old shirts too old and worn for anything else – while their daily clothes, which were also their Sunday clothes, were carefully and painstakingly prepared. No 'one on, one off, one in the wash' for most of us.

What people wore depended on age, sex or status. I seem to remember the majority of men wore dark suits... or did they? When I generalise, memory makes all trips flow into one, so in my mind they all wore dark suits – with the order of service from the last funeral in a pocket, or possibly if they'd been lucky a programme from a rugby international – and of course Gillard would show everyone his programme from the Wales/All Blacks game of 1905 – again! It would come to a sad end one day. And more than one pocket held a discreet bottle opener...

Waistcoats were adorned with a father's, grandfather's or even great-grandfather's watch chain. Alas, more than one did not have a watch so the chain ended in a large washer, the watch having long been pawned.

Highly polished black boots at one end and an often equally shiny bowler hat at the other completed the attire. Again, the bowler was rarely the original property of the wearer, but had been handed down. Despite blood ties, head sizes did not run in families so some hats were perched absurdly like thimbles on a snooker ball while others sank over ears nearly down to the shoulders. A sudden glance to the side by such a wearer would often leave the hat facing forward as the head actually revolved inside the brim. It was generally agreed that too big was better than too small and too large could be padded with strips of newspaper which in itself could produce amusing results on a wet day. But, remember, it never rained on Coal Trip day.

The smell of mothballs, soap and Brylcreem was overpowering! Students – a few home from 'coll' for the 'vac' wore sports coats, light trousers and cravats… causing more than a few comments from the more conservative element present.

The rugby team, resplendent in their brand new blazers and greys, did have the grace to look ashamed.

And what of the fairer sex?

All manner of finery!

Bright, floral dresses or skirts, colourful blouses, hats galore and all manner of hairstyles, all created in someone's kitchen – not for them the luxury of a hairdresser.

All memories of hardships were put aside for one glorious day of freedom.

As boys we had grey – or was it khaki? – shorts, your own if you were lucky or, depending on your place in the family, a big brother's or a cut down pair of dad's: as long as the arse wasn't out of them it was O.K. It was bad enough having the arse out of your own trousers, but having the arse out of someone else's; that was a disgrace.

On our feet we had ¾ grey socks – just like William – or was it white ankle socks? While a few of us had sandals, most of us sported 'daps'. These were black canvas shoes with rubber soles and either an elasticated instep or laces. These would be worn throughout the summer, getting sweatier and sweatier, and smellier and smellier. I always thought 'dap' was a Welsh word – slang – but still Welsh. In the navy, and later at college, I heard of similar footwear called sandshoes, plimsolls, pumps or sports shoes, but to us they were always 'daps'. I was recently disappointed to learn that 'dap' was really an acronym for Dunlop Air Pillow. I hope it's not true. 'Dap' sounds as if it SHOULD be Welsh.

Our heads were topped with the remains of our summer haircut – very, very short, with a quiff – a skinhead today, but we called it a Crongie. Again, only recently I discovered the name came from a South African general called Cronje – pronounced Cronhay – who, sporting such a haircut, had his picture in many British newspapers during the Boer War. Whether we copied the style, or the name, or both, I'm not sure.

Eric stood out like a sore thumb, not that he was poorly or untidily dressed, he was just, well, different. Usual beret, then a gleaming white three-piece suit – 'knocked up in Port Said you know' with sandals, no socks. And, oh yes, an umbrella. But it can't have been raining – can it? Larry was immaculate in a yellow and green striped blazer, sporting what I later discovered to be his beloved Regiment's tie, a pair of light trousers which were undoubtedly the baggiest I have ever seen; two-tone, brown leather shoes, topped off with, of all things, a straw boater. I'm not sure he didn't have a banjo and a tennis racquet – he looked like something from a P. G. Wodehouse story. And of course, they had their trawling bags, also a great leather satchel apiece held together with string and faith, each big enough to hold a small library. And if that wasn't enough, they had their trawling pram! It wasn't empty; it contained Sailor's wonderful gramophone and his current collection of records.

Sailor bless him, his trip paid-for every year by very popular subscription, was to provide music on the beach. He made me even happier, if that were at all possible, by presenting me with a miniature trawling bag of my very own. It was a simple canvas holdall with an adjustable shoulder strap embroidered with my name and a rather explicit mermaid (complete with comb, mirror and long flowing hair, not long enough I'm pleased to say to cover her two finest attributes... however... 'I'd keep that fine illustration discreetly hidden my boy... don't use it to take your bible to chapel! I think it better if you store it in the shop... your Boppa may not appreciate the maid's appearance.') Eric later told me that Sailor, when he heard I was going on the trip, had stayed up all night sewing it.

'It will be better than last year old friend,' said Larry.

'A broken leg would be better than last year,' was the quiet reply. When Eric had returned to live in Penddawn he'd offered to run the pub for the day of the trip, a totally pointless offer as those not on the trip were either dead, ill or indifferent! It was an offer Huw had no trouble in turning down. 'I'd rather invite Crippen to dinner and ask him to season the cawl. Thank you very much all the same.'

Normally their 'duties' consisted of sitting on chairs in front of the Penddawn Arms, to keep an eye on things while

67

contentedly drinking their beer in the sun. The previous year the Dark Lady had arrived... Larry had just gone for a wander around the deserted streets, quite needless really, but that was Larry.

She went first to the shop... then to the pub... where Eric, basking in the sun, was caught totally unawares. Spotting his unwelcome visitor he fled. She had stood quietly for a few minutes studying the crate of flagons. Then, delicately, she had opened each bottle and gently, and as he later recounted, had almost tenderly poured the contents down the gutter. We learned this, because, to her eternal delight, Boppa saw it all and lovingly recounted the tale in full detail to each and every one who'd listen. Finishing her account with tears of mirth rolling down her cheeks. 'That poor mistreated woman skipped and sang all the way back to the station, while those two were crying like babies. Oh, it did my Christian heart good it did. God is not mocked you know.'

Everyone sympathised, well, nearly everyone, but all agreed it really was bloody funny!

And finally you could bet a year's pay or more realistically a year's dole that everyone had on... CLEAN UNDERWEAR.

Regardless of age or sex be they frillies or long johns, by golly they were clean.

I know all writers say this, but I swear it's true.

Does my memory play tricks?

I think not.

I hope not.

Suddenly, the buses.

You could hear them long before you saw them. They pulled up at the bunker, coughing, spluttering, spewing smoke and fumes, a fleet of mainly single but with two double-deckers, and, from somewhere, a charabanc… known fondly and not so fondly as the "toast rack". Possibly it could be described as a bench with an engine, topped by its driver… 'Barmy Banister'. There's need for an explanation about that nickname. He'd originally been called 'Stairs' – very subtle and original I'm sure. 'Stairs', as he was, had spent all his life with horses, first as a boy on one of the last farms in the valley, then as a haulier working underground with pit ponies, and finally as a delivery man for the local dairy. On his retirement, 'Stairs' had been introduced to the internal combustion engine by his granddaughter's husband, who ran a small garage. This new skill he'd grabbed with both hands. He'd shown the greatest enthusiasm, but this enthusiasm was coupled with a total lack of skill. However, he took up his new trade with both hands, literally. He drove occasionally for his son-in-law's bus company and it was something he relished, but sometimes, while on a run to Pontypridd or Cardiff, his mind would drift away and he'd back underground, or on his farm. At such times he'd forget where he was or what he was doing and as he approached a junction or bus stop he would, to the great consternation and great fear of his passengers, pull sharply on the wheel and yell 'WHOA MY BEAUTY!' It wasn't long before he was known as 'Barmy'!

'Thank God I'm not going in the 'toast rack', was a silent and not-so-silent prayer uttered by many. The buses were another thing. You felt that if they'd been offered to Napoleon's army in full retreat from Moscow the soldiers would have taken one look... and carried on walking. Eric's comment of, 'God, I'd look after horses better' turned out to be almost prophetic.

Each bus had in charge of it a COMMITTEE official... each clutching, with a great deal of self-importance, a clipboard with a list of names of who was travelling on HIS bus – yes, HIS in capital letters. Never mind who actually owned the vehicle, the COMMITTEE had hired it – THEY owned it, if only for the day and no chance of a 'her', much less in capitals, having any say in the matter.

We were divided into three groups: children, up to the age of fourteen, self-explanatory, on the double-deckers.

Then: drinkers on the so-called 'wet' buses.

Then non-drinkers – known behind their backs as 'Deacons' – on the dry.

Take my word for it, the dry buses were DRY! You had more chance of a drink in a pub on a Sunday in the most Bible-Black (thank you again, Dylan) part of Wales than a drink on a dry bus. Each bus marshal – as they liked to be called – would check off his passengers. There was no mercy. If your name was on the list; that was your bus. The dry buses had many a hapless husband, sweetheart or fiancé forced to accompany a partner, watching almost tearfully as single friends literally poured onto the wet transport.

A mighty cheer went up as the newly married captain of the Penddawn Rugby team decided he didn't want to be with his nearest and dearest on a dry bus made a spirited dash to the oasis of a wet one, only to be caught and dragged back by his new in-laws – now his out-laws – to his stony-faced, white-lipped nearest and dearest... I suppose if he'd been a back he might have made it, but a forward... no chance.

The twenty or so travellers on the open-sided, topless charabanc were the students who were given no choice, a few odd volunteers – very few, very odd – the rest chosen by lot.

The last three to get on it were Eric, Larry, Sailor and, of course, the pram, complete with gramaphone. Eric and Larry's late decision to go on the trip meant that they could not afford to be choosy. Getting the pram loaded was a job and three-quarters. Ever tried getting a large pram with a fragile precious load onto a charabanc? Like putting an obstinate pit pony onto a roller skate was the analogy I especially liked. In the finest tradition of the Royal Navy, Sailor, three sheets to the wind, was standing rigidly to attention shouting, 'Make it so! Lift the port side up, no the port side you deaf buggers. Make it so!' at the hilarious attempts. As it and Eric were finally pulled aboard, Larry turned, raised his boater aloft and cried out, 'Hail, Caesar. We who are about to die salute you!'

A few of the students not on the toast rack and some other responsible adults were pressed into caring for us on the double-deckers. Many families of course stayed as groups, but some were happy to split up, to re-unite of course at Tenby. And a few like me were on our own; not that anyone was on their own on the coal trip.

It was like Christmas.

We all had a bottle of Mr Evans' pop, an orange, an apple, bar of chocolate, a penny… or was that actually Christmas? As well as this there was the multitude of foodstuffs provided from home. Boppa, bless her, had done me proud. Everything was home-made, of course, with cakes, pies, great slabs of toffee and packets and packets of grease-proofed or newspaper-covered sandwiches, fruit, brown paper bags of biscuits – broken ones were cheaper – and lashings of home-made ginger beer. I'd defy Enid Blyton or Arthur Ransome to describe the feast. Mind you, I had tried ginger beer once and found it positively revolting. Mr. Evan's Dandelion and Burdock was my favourite.

It was better than Christmas.

The wet buses were already loaded with crates of bottled beers, brown ale, light, mild, dark and, of course, the flagons: Felinfoel's cans hadn't reached our part of the world yet, so the beer was all in bottles. Bus marshals distributed spending money, along with peppermints, cigarettes, or tobacco – pipe, rolling, twist and the snuff users had their nicotine habit satisfied – and other goodies – more to travellers on the dry buses – and allocation was meticulously fair, to the last farthing or humbug. Those who, for whatever reason, were unable to make the trip had their share as exact as if they were there on the day.

All supplied foodstuffs came from our corner shop, 'Charlie's', a real 'Open-All-Hours' establishment. Charlie, the owner, swore he gave the committee fair prices and a good discount, but there were doubts. Many people bemoan the loss of the corner shop, but today as I trundle my trolley around Tesco or wherever at least I know my private life won't be analysed by the manager, his wife and assorted cronies, as it was at 'Charlie's', either by the man himself, his wife or one of the regular harpies who hung out there. You'd be clutching your Saturday penny eager to spend it, burning hot in your hand and you'd stand and wait and wait and wait, while birth, marriage and death would enfold in front of you… especially births and dates of marriages… at least today when I'm queuing at an impersonal checkout you know the poor soul at the till is generally doing their best and will serve you as soon as you arrive. At Charlie's… you'd be ignored while adults had priority. He enjoyed the war and the control it gave him over people, the bastard.

Was any man dismayed?

Well, yes there was. To be fair it wasn't all sweetness and light: a number of people thought the trip 'ungodly'. Too many people were having a good time and there was too much emphasis on the 'demon drink'. Many discussions were held behind drawn curtains. Some had a genuine dislike in seeing people enjoying themselves and if alcohol was involved…

The Daniel at Bellshazzar's Feast was Y Parchedig Charteris Templar Evans. Y Parch., or Reverend Evans, clothed in black, with a mane of shoulder length white hair, five foot nothing, remained a presence, a personality, a living embodiment of Lloyd George's suggestion that 'In Wales we measure a man from the neck up'. He was standing stock-still, glowering at the happy throng, looking, I imagine, like Pharaoh observing the Exodus, grasping his walking stick… walking stick? That's like calling the Ark Royal 'a boat'. It was a great staff of oak, a foot taller than him, bound in brass at the bottom, topped with a mighty ram's horn worthy of Gabriel himself. Legend had it that it once belonged to the great Dr. William Price himself.

He was a familiar sight striding through the streets, the sound of his staff crashing on the pavements announcing his presence long before he came into view. Children would hide; doors would close, milk turn and sheep miscarry.

He was a deeply, deeply religious man, but like so many he didn't seem to enjoy or get comfort from his beliefs. He suffered them. He lived by the simple rule – simple to him – of 'NO TOLERANCE'.

I'd seen grown men shaking after one of his sermons.

Alcohol was his greatest concern. Yes, some drank some of the time, a few, a very few drank a lot of the time. Most, however drank very little, and cost was for many a problem. Did you buy five Woodbines and share them, or did you make a pint last all night? And of course being 'chapel' was a very strong reason for abstention. There was for many the pull of the pew over the pull of the pulled pint.

Today, as I wrestle with my alcohol demons, I wonder if the old parch had the right idea.

He stood this glad day…

Glaring. Silent.

He was not going to read the writing on the wall, oh no, he was going to carve the words himself in letters of fire.

Raising what was recognised as his staff of office he struck it to the ground.

Crash!

'Sinners!'

Crash!
'Fornicators.'

Crash!

'Drunkards.'

Crash!

'Adulterers.'

'The hottest fires of Hell are yet now being prepared!'

I think you get the general picture.

The first time I saw – and heard – this performance it had sent me scurrying off to find a dictionary, which didn't make me any the wiser. Eric gave me better definitions… adding 'unfortunately my boy I have a "nap" hand of those sins the good parch lists.'

Eric, being very high church, was ignored by Evans. He was doomed, but those of us who were 'chapel'… we had some chance of salvation.

Interestingly Larry professed to be an atheist after his experiences in the Great War. Much later he told me he was a Buddhist. As he said, 'It was easier to say I was a non-believer, not exactly popular in certain quarters, but not altogether unacceptable or unknown in a socialist area with a tradition of freethinking. But Buddhist? I'd rather have admitted to being a Lutheran to Torquemada while he was toasting bread by the fire.'

ENOUGH! Let's be on our way. And with a great series of cheers we were off. Up through the valley we went... the singing started straight away. On our bus was heard 'She'll be Coming Round the Mountain', songs from *Snow White*, 'Green Grow The Rushes' and others, so many, many others and, of course, hymns and arias, all verses, all in Welsh, Italian or German, and not only half-remembered but fully remembered, 'Cwm Rhondda', in English with 'Feed Me Now and Evermore' not, 'Till I want No More', that meaningless chorus that is bellowed today. How different to today and Max Boyce's 'Ten Thousand Instant Christians!'

We journeyed through the reaches of the upper valley with its posh houses, and their larger than normal terraces, with all manner of additions, usually in the form of pillars and posts making up a grandiose porch built in the style known facetiously as 'Baronial Rhondda'.

The first travel-sickness bucket was soon used, before we had even passed onto the mountain road that had been built only ten years or so previously by a 'voluntary' work-force of the unemployed.

Up... up... up... the buses crawling painfully to the top. In some cases the marshals were literally pushing people off to lighten the load... 'You're young enough... we'll wait at the top!' But in some cases it was the human ballasts who had to wait for their bus to catch them up!

At last then the summit, although we'd been travelling a bare half an hour or so everyone got off to stretch their legs, and in the case of the more enthusiastic revellers – seek a secluded spot, a difficult task as all the trees had been long stripped from mountain sides to provide wood for the maw of the great god coal. It was said a ton of wood was left underground for every ton of coal taken overground.

To me it was the top of the world... the reservoirs... Vale of Neath, the Brecon Beacons stretched out... if James Hilton had seen it his paradise would have been right there, not the Himalayas. The last of the unathletic load-lighteners arrived, bright red, sweating, swearing, puffing and panting but laughing, already the odd collar and tie dispensed with.

A group of older men – I suppose most were sixty plus – sat quietly on their haunches in the classic miner's rest position, clearing their chests with the aid of a Woodbine. Llew hawked a great gob of phlegm into the road. 'If they could collect all the dust in my chest the whole bloody valley could have a month in Tenby,' he spluttered.

I edged over. Llew was usually good for a story...

'Pity old Twenty isn't here to enjoy this. He should be here today,' someone said. Everyone nodded or made noises of agreement. Gareth, 'Twenty' Williams, Llew's old mining and drinking buddy, had died a few months previously.

'Aye,' said Llew, 'It wasn't the dust killed him though, or his heart, despite what the coroner said... It was that...' Llew's chapel background was at conflict with his feelings ... 'It was that... "blighter" – chapel won – RTD Jones.'

And that is the cue for another story, and today is the day. It will occupy the time for the long old journey to Tenby; it takes all of three hours. So as the buses finally roll down the mountain towards Neath, to Carmarthen, St. Clears and on to Tenby – with no toilets on our buses, so there'll be a few stops, but not much traffic only narrow, twisty roads. It's a long old trip so let's have the story of...

THE RETURN OF RTD, OR
THE STORY OF THE SCOREBOARD

The inquest into the death of Gareth 'Twenty' Williams was straightforward enough.

'Verdict.'

'Death by natural causes.'

'Thank you.'

'Next, please.'

But, the dry verdict didn't please everyone.

No there was no Wimsey or Poirot shouting 'Murder Most Foul!'

No, there was no suspicion about his death or a casting of doubt on the cause of death; but there lingered the question of not how he'd died but… but…

Why?

Llew had no doubts at all.

'Oh yes,' he was heard to say. 'He died because of his heart; it was his heart all right, broken by RTD, as surely as if he'd been shot, stabbed or strangled.'

Well, I suppose it would be better if I begin at the beginning…

It all began when Robert RTD Davis came back to Penddawn. He too, like Hywel May, had left the Valley to seek his fortune, and, he too came back a wealthy man and, by golly, he didn't half want people to know just how wealthy he was.

But, for reasons to be unfolded he'd never been popular before he left, his somewhat shady departure being seen by many as no bad thing. Now he was back, obviously very well off, to become in time even more disliked. I hasten to add that jealousy over his good fortune was not the reason.

For a start his nickname. Since his schooldays he'd been known as 'D' just a natural shortening of his given name, David, you'd think. But it was believed to be short for 'Devious'. Can you call an initial a 'nickname'? Anyway, RTD was how he had become known in Penddawn, throughout the Valley and far beyond, but, those initials stood for:

Rob, not as in Robert… but rob as in steal.

The.

Dead.

His family had always been well off by any standards; by our standards they were veritable millionaires. They'd owned a coal mine, small but nevertheless profitable. Then at the turn of the century, not this one, the last one, as could happen, the coal literally ran out, the family were left broke. His brothers, graduates, degrees in engineering, no problem for them obtaining work, but Rob, as he still was then, had no 'paper' to help him along. There was talk of him going to an overseas college in the Dominions where it was believed, totally erroneously, that academic standards were lower. He seemed all set to go to Canada, but a rumour circulated about forged references. His family influence had finally run out. He was forced to take a job underground, getting his hands dirty which was not to his liking. Oh no, getting his hands… dirty… not to his liking at all… ach y fi… so it was.

With the mines in full production RTD found himself working in the 'Co-op', the name by which our colliery was known. Almost immediately he had a 'stall', a much envied 'place of his own', which he worked shift and shift about with his brother-in-law, John. How he'd got his own stall in the first place, as young and inexperienced as he was – and such a prize place to work at that – was a source of annoyance to many, but it was no real mystery. Remember, well some of you may remember, a miner then was paid by the amount of coal he could cut, so easily-mined stalls were very important (no stalls were 'easy') but some were more productive than others. Such stalls were much prized and usually only given to the best and most senior colliers, but there were exceptions, ways and means....

So when 'devout' Anglican, pillar-of-the-church – a warden no less – and union hating Rob started attending chapel – not just any chapel mind you, but the same one that some very 'Fed' senior officials from the 'Co-op' attended – and was seen walking down the main road in broad daylight, hand-in-hand with the daughter of one of those officials.... She was ten years older than him and getting more than a little desperate... it was a foregone conclusion. It was said that Davis could have taught the Vicar of Bray a few things.

Anyway, one day when he came on shift, there'd been a roof fall and John, poor sod, had been killed, so it goes, one of the countless killed or maimed in one of numerous underground accidents. This was a death covered by the local press, but which wouldn't rate a paragraph in any of the nationals. He was a victim unknown outside his own community, whose butties would lose pay for the time to take him home, and later to attend the funeral. Yes, the price of coal, indeed. Anyway, John had just filled a dram and chalked his 'mark' on it ready for its journey to the surface where Billy 'Chwarae Teg' would weigh it, and in due course a payment would have been made. RTD reached the stall just after the tragedy and rubbed out John's mark... and substituted his own...

Now, you'd have thought he'd have been lynched, at the very least. Of course he was called all the scum-names under the sun. I'm sure that Nye Bevan himself heard the 'lower than vermin' comment in Tredegar and stored it for future use.

RTD swore – justifiably? – that it wasn't so. He and John went 50/50 on all they earned. He made the very valid point that if he hadn't changed marks the coal would have been 'lost' and put in the pockets of 'those pigs of owners, instead of in the purse of my dear wife's widowed sister.' What he said was true, but, there was, in many minds, an underlying doubt. There was always the 'but'. For some time he was called 'Rob the Dead' and it was some time before it was softened to RTD.

The final blow to any sort of reputation he may have had came in 1911, after the Tonypandy Riots. The strike had dragged on causing great suffering and hardship for months.

In the September came a rugby match between the police and striking miners. It was, I suppose, a match comparable with a certain football game played in December 1914 in France, only this game was not as friendly. The police were the 'Mets', what we'd call a paramilitary force today, an army of occupation, who, with the military, remained in the Valley to 'Keep the Peace', after the riots and until the trials of the ring leaders.

Well it so happened the police were a man short for their team. RTD happened to be one of the many spectators and despite some pretty harsh looks and not a few harsher comments he was quite happy to turn out for the police. That in itself was almost acceptable. On field all rivalries were generally put aside. Rugby was rugby and striking was striking, so, let's win by fair means, make it 15-a-side and don't give them a chance afterwards to moan about being a man short. 'Besides RTD is useless; he'll hinder them and help us!'

By all accounts it was a well-matched, close-fought game; no quarter was asked or given. Tackling was hard and I'm told the front row tussle was quite something. The miners were leading by a try to nil, when, in the dying seconds, Llew the miners' wing misjudged a clearance kick which bounced straight into the arms of police wing RTD who was in spotless strip despite the muddy conditions. RTD thought he was standing well out of harm's way but acting on some instinct, dropped a superb goal, his instinct being to get rid of the ball as quickly as possible! The shout of congratulations from the police captain was followed by the ref's whistling for no-side. Bear in mind the date... an unconverted try was worth 3 points... and a drop goal was worth four. To say RTD wasn't popular is a slight understatement.

Later in the Penddawn Arms the losers had to buy their opposite number in the winning team a half pint, which they could ill afford. Few of them had tasted a pint for many months and to buy one for a policeman. It was not as though they could afford to buy a drink for themselves.

It must have hurt Llew somewhat to buy a drink for RTD. I think he'd have preferred to have given his daughter's virginity to Winston Churchill, and Llew was from Tonypandy, where Churchill sent in the soldiers.

I suppose the final straw for RTD came when his wife left him; she disappeared with a policeman, the very copper who RTD had replaced in the epic match a few weeks previously. Now, if truth be told, her departure did not upset him too greatly. He called her his 'Beloved Betty', but by all accounts she was a real harridan. What hurt was the public disgrace of being cuckolded, by a policeman and, even worse, they left with his savings! Which caused the greater grief is hard to say. People debated long and hard whether it was his feelings, his wife or his money he wept for.

Eric, with his literary bent, acted out enthusiastically in the bar of the Penddawn Arms a part from *The Merchant of Venice*; Shylock's reaction to his daughter's elopement, with his money.

'My daughter! O my ducats. O my daughter.' (Act II Scene VIII if you are interested).

His performance earned him a look of disapproval from Larry.

Meanwhile Llew was to be seen walking around with a smile for some considerable time, and would tell anyone who'd listen, 'Well, well, well, you see while he was dropping a goal she was dropping her knickers! Well, well, well.' I think Llew thought it was worth a half pint.

I suppose RTD felt he had nothing left in Penddawn, nothing to lose by a move, and everything to gain. So it was off to Philadelphia in the morning. Actually he did a moonlight flit and went to Chicago, but that's by the by. And now some twenty-odd years later, he was back. He'd never fitted in then and now, on his return, he fitted in, at least for a while, even less.

Now, as you know, Hywel May had come back to Penddawn a wealthy man, but Hywel, bless him, had never flaunted his wealth. Yes, he'd bought the houses but he had lived simply enough with April; he was always a Valley boy at heart. He'd have a pint in the pub, yarn with old mates; a visitor to his house was guaranteed a welcome, a tea, a beer or even, heaven forbid, in those far off days, a coffee!

Everything about RTD exuded wealth, he wore magnificent double-breasted suits, shirts of many colours adorned with bright green ties – 'My lucky colour boys' – and bright, shiny, ornately-tooled cowboy boots with quite a nice heel, and, believe it or not, a cowboy hat. Yes, he certainly cut a fine figure of a successful man, nay, a successful American – an effect somewhat lost when he opened his mouth. His accent jumped from Chicago to Cardiff via Cwmparc and back in a single sentence, with a mixture of idioms that had to be heard to be believed. Eccentrics and their foibles were generally tolerated, no, more than tolerated, enjoyed, relished even, Eric and Larry being good examples, but it was their way, how they were. With RTD it was sheer ostentation.

RTD had bought a huge mansion of a place, 'Park Manor' no less, down the Vale. Indeed it was in Cowbridge, so 'Baronial Rhondda' indeed.

Few were invited to his palatial home, the grand house, nay, manor where he and his new wife – American – held court to the chosen ones. One day a few Penddawn friends, no contemporaries – he had no friends – while at Cowbridge Market called in totally uninvited for, let's be honest, a good old Valley 'nose'. They included Eric who was 'trawling'.

'Boys', they later reported. 'A bloody butler answered the door, there were maids everywhere and his wife... we'd have had a better welcome if we'd been Medicis at a Borgia wedding. She couldn't get us out quick enough.'

People shook their heads; common courtesy costing nothing.

As RTD took us to the door he said, 'Bye boys, sorry and all that, but don't call again…'

Eric who'd known the 'Beloved Betty', told an appreciative audience, 'He's the only man I know who marries the Wicked Witch of the West, manages to escape, and then marries the Wicked Witch of the East!!! I'd love,' he continued, 'to have thrown a bucket of water over her and watched her bloody melt. Or even better, landed Park Manor on top of both their stupid heads!' I didn't appreciate the 'Oz' references until I – and millions of others – fell in love with Judy a year or so later and was able to see for myself exactly what he meant.

But, on his visits to the Valley it was all 'Hail Fellows Well Met' and he would become the worst, patronising sort of bastard. On his first visit he was chauffeur-driven to Castle, then took a two-minute tram ride to Penddawn. He strolled into the pub as 'one of the boys', look you, and bought beer for everyone all night.

Fine, on his first visit Hywel had done the same to celebrate his return. Not many men will turn down a free pint or two and 'Thank you very much.' But RTD had done it again and again, dropping all nonsense of trams, taking the bloody Rolls Royce to the door of the pub. And proud men without pennies began to feel… I don't know, small or insignificant. Obviously there were some more than happy to accept this manna, but many… they may not have had work, but by God they had their pride.

'What's he trying to prove?'

'What does he want?'

'What's he after…? The devious old sod…'

It was soon to become apparent what he was after; something at the very heart of the entire community… the devious old sod…it would soon be revealed… he WAS a devious old sod.

And the question was asked, where did he get his oh so obvious wealth from?

As I mentioned earlier there'd been silly stories of how dear old Hywel had made his money. No one thought it was anything really sinister; it was a good subject for an hour's yarning and that was it… similar tales were rife about RTD.

Everybody knew that he'd gone to America. The coal areas of the States were obvious target destinations for armies of miners looking for work; nothing in the Old World, so let's try the New. But RTD had wound up in Chicago, in that city's infamous meat trade, employed at one of the vast, vast slaughter houses, disgusting, filthy work even by mining standards and that is certainly saying something. (If you are really interested read Sinclair Lewis *The Concrete Jungle*. If that doesn't put you off burgers! However...)

But Chicago... the name conjured up (in the creative and in the, it must be said, somewhat over-imaginative minds of Penddawn) a world of gangsters, bootlegging and tommy-guns... and to this was added the fact that RTD's new wife was undoubtedly of Italian extraction... the cinema certainly had a lot to answer for.

His comment of having left America 'for reasons of my health...' was seized upon...

'He didn't want a pair of concrete overshoes...'

'He came back before he woke up dead...'

'He'd have slept with the fishes'... or... 'slept with the crachons,' as local idiom would have expressed it.

Oh yes, very fond of the cinema were the folk of Penddawn.

It was openly bandied about that Capone himself had heard his nickname and immediately hired him. Then, realising what a liability he had on his hands he paid him off with a wife and dowry so as a 'family' member it ensured he kept his mouth shut.

A little far-fetched? Perhaps. In RTD's case I think so, but, and it is a BIG 'but' read John Morgan's book *No Gangster More Bold*. Capone's 'right-hand man' was indeed Welsh, a Mr Llewellyn Morgan Humphries, known as the 'Hump'… whose cousin now sits in the House of Lords… Dafydd Wigley if you are at all interested.

One day RTD paid a visit to the book shop, where the three of us were sitting in companionable silence; and, it must be said, companionable darkness during another 'power cut', when RTD blustered in. Now, as I've said, 'power cuts' were not unusual and were an accepted part of the way of things. When RTD came in it was different. He seemed even to me openly contemptuous of the shop. It may have been shabby and it may have been in darkness, but it was much loved by many.

He casually picked up a book, a Penguin, *Tarka the Otter*, and pointedly bent over the candle to look at it. 'Tuppence? Seems a good price.' The original price was, I may add, purely out of interest you understand, 6d… old money that is… 2.5p in today's excuse for a currency. He took a thick roll of bank notes from his hip pocket ('arse pocket' in our coarse Valley patois). The sight of so much cash struck us all dumb. Licking his fingers, he peeled a 10 shilling note from the wad and placed it on the table… you could have cut the silence with a knife.

'Here you go guys, don't worry your asses making change.'

His 'American' accent, combined with what was left of his Welsh and taken together with the slang, grated.

Eric closed his eyes… ten bob was more than they took most weeks.

Larry rose magnificently to the occasion, his long face as impassive as an Easter Island monolith. 'I'm afraid the donkeys are busy out the back at the moment so we won't worry them. However, thank you so much for your generous offer; but please, take Mr Williamson's fine text as a welcome-home present from us all.'

They had pride those two.

RTD picked up the note, returned it to its roll and walked out in a silence only broken by the squeaking of his magnificent boots. *Tarka* was left on the table… Eric picked it up and threw it to me. 'Here you are,' he said. 'Don't worry about bringing it back; just enjoy it as I know you will.' I have it still. Larry looked at him across the table. 'Were you friends at school?' Eric snorted. 'Contemporaries, hardly friends, he had no bloody friends, hangers-on and 'Yes Men' but friends… not a single bloody one.'

Eric then began a long speech – almost a diatribe. Unlike a lot of articulate men he did not love the sound of his own voice. I reproduce here as, accurately as memory allows, his words, many of which passed over me but later I was able to make sense of them... anyway, here we go, or rather here he goes...

'He had no friends... but always wanted to be popular... he could not see why he was unpopular. He wanted to be liked, but it didn't help that he was a snob of the first order. He wanted to be liked, but couldn't go about it in the right way. Then, as now, he'd try to buy his way in – now it's beer, then it was sweets.

Basically he had this enormous chip on his shoulder – wealthy parents, two elder brothers highly successful in surveying and engineering and it was anticipated he would do equally as well academically – alas his talents lay elsewhere. He, through no fault of his own, just didn't have it; whatever 'it' is. It didn't help he was bone idle; always on the lookout for short cuts. Why should he work? He had everything, it would all, sooner or later, one way or another, come to him.

Money was all-important to him; he was obsessed with money and possessions. It was his sole criterion of how he judged people; money and property, worldly goods, nothing else counted. He felt inferior to his brothers, no doubt, so he would always try to prove his superiority over those he considered inferior, materialistically.

He had everything any child could want, or even dream of… bike, train set (clockwork of course), a football and proper football boots, you name it he had it, all new of course; same with his clothes, none of Mam's knitting for him… hand-me downs? You must be joking, all his stuff was shop-bought and let me tell you, none of your Ponty market stuff for Mrs. Davies' little boy, oh no. Howells, in Cardiff of course…'

Eric's voice was rising. 'His vile, spiteful, comments to kids in 'hand-me-downs' had to be heard to be believed. Never mind that their mother was a widow struggling to bring up six of us on a pittance of a pension…'

'Us?' from Larry. 'Got a bit personal did it?'

'Yes, it bloody well did get personal… for by God if you had something… he could with a single contemptuous word destroy any pleasure you had from a simple home-made toy crafted with love, not bought with cash. If by chance you had something just that little bit special or that little bit different, he'd covet it. He'd pour on the charm and smooth and grind and grease you down relentlessly until you surrendered it to him not really knowing why you had done so. Something he didn't want or need – he just didn't want YOU to have it.'

'Got to you a bit then,' said Larry softly, a statement not question.

'He could always find a weak spot which he would work on. Anything you had he'd criticise and any one you admired he'd acidly belittle… on and on and on… until at last you'd react, and you'd be lucky to match him verbally. He'd shred you my friends, obscenity was a waste of time, and if you tried to be physical… he'd won… he could hurt you physically…, a very clever, very skilful bully. Later, as an adult, he could walk into a room and effortlessly suck out any light, warmth or happiness there, cheerfully skipping out, job done! He would leave behind a vacuum… if misery, frustration and anger can be called a vacuum. He was never able to resist a jibe or a gloat especially when his target was unable to retaliate. He was always the spectre at any feast. A sad, lonely, vicious, spiteful boy who has become what he is; I am sure he hasn't changed… watch him because "the child is father of the man".' He would never do anything for anyone without an ulterior motive. Mark my words: he is after something.'

'Right,' abruptly from Larry, 'let's go and have a pint. Rod, mind the shop please.'

He strode purposefully from the shop. Eric, after a few deep and heartfelt sighs, followed. The effect was somewhat spoilt by their return barely a minute later… they had no money and the long-suffering Huw had stopped their slate.

We sat for a long time in compatible silence leaving me to thoughts I did not understand, and *Tarka*, a book I cannot now, 60 years later, pick up without remembering that afternoon, and how prophetic Eric's words were to prove.

It was soon discovered that RTD's scheme was quite simply to take over Penddawn Rugby Football Club. He knew our weak spot and saw how he could exploit it. Sport was popular for recreation and we had our fair share of parks and even swimming pools: yes, even in the 30s they existed. OK, they were open air and pretty basic but we had them and we were proud of them and the simple fact we had them was more than many similar areas in Britain could boast. I don't think I met in later years anyone from any other British industrial areas who enjoyed the number of recreational facilities that we had.

Importantly, sport could provide an escape from the hardship of the daily grind for survival if only for a few hours a week either playing or supporting your local team… and of course there was boxing… a sure way to wealth and fame. I should say that every village, town and city in those dark days had their great boxing hope, the old adage being that the best fighters were the hungry ones.

Alas, it was the hard way indeed. 'Many were called but few were chosen'… and very few were chosen. Many were the broken down old men, and not so old, who tried to fight their way to fame and fortune. They would work all day, existing on a pretty scant diet, then be fighting two, three, four, even five times a week in what was, in many cases, legalised thuggery. There was only the thinnest protection over twisted knuckles, and it was a mere step up from the days of bare fists' courage. Bugger the Queen Of Marquesbury, whoever the hell he was, until after one fight too many they'd be dumped by their manager outside the scene of their latest and alas last failure; to seek a new hero to take on the road to success, while their former rising star would be left to manage as best he could. If they were lucky they had a return ticket and possibly a few begrudged pennies and were then forced to rely on families and mates for future support, as all too often they'd be unemployable apart from the most menial of jobs given for charity. Even the successful ones, often badly advised and a target for every 'conman' in town, would have that one fight too many.

Huw, bless him, had once upon a time 'employed' Tarw Barnett, a great-hearted but now broken boxer down on his luck. His job was to walk the valley putting up posters of forthcoming events, anything from, ironically, boxing matches to details of choir or band practices. He offered him ten bob a week, or... all the beer he could drink. Tarw, not as daft as he looked, took the beer option... Ten bob equals 120 old pennies; a pint then cost 3 old pennies, so you do the maths... After a week of this deal Tarw was on a flat rate of ten bob. To add insult to injury, Tarw wasn't exactly the greatest of scholars, not helped by eyes covered in scar tissue, so he put many posters upside down and Huw had to pay someone to discreetly follow him around and put them up properly!

But people still spoke and indeed still speak with awe of many who did fight their way to success. Jimmy Wilde, the 'Ghost with the Hammer in his Hand', the world flyweight champion of the 20s, 101 fights undefeated... and of course... Tommy Farr... who could forget that night in 1937 against Joe Louis, The Brown Bomber himself, for the Richest Prize in Sport, the world heavyweight title? Who could forget that night... well I could for one, as I fell asleep waiting for the big moment, but that is by the by.

Anyway...

The great love for most was our rugby club, The Penddawn All Stars, who were known for reasons lost in the mystery of time as 'The Giraffes'. Apparently their jerseys originally had been a dark yellow and brown, but after one disastrous wash when the colours had run and become strangely mottled they were given the nickname and it stuck. The club was enjoying a period of considerable success. The club and players were a glorious ray of light for the entire community of Penddawn, people who'd never been to a game in their lives would turn up to support 'The Boys'. Even those who didn't turn up could remember every detail of each and every game vividly and would be there Monday morning with the best of them commenting on each and every scrum and lineout. There must have been 5,000 at some games. Now there was talk of becoming 'A FIRST CLASS CLUB'!

You must remember at this time there were no leagues or cups to play for. All games were 'friendly' and of course, all teams were equal; but, some matches were considerably friendlier than others, and some teams were considerably more equal than others. The Welsh Rugby Union had pretty well decided who were first class and who were second… and ne'r the twain would meet. So teams like Cardiff, Swansea and Newport were first class and would remain so with all the privileges that brought. We, and other valleys' teams like Ystrad, Treorchy and so on were second class and there we would remain. Occasionally, a top team would send players for a charity or a testimonial game. Most, if not all of their players came from Valleys' teams and the quality players would naturally make their way to the stars, and no one blamed them. Why play for Penddawn when you could play for Cardiff? There was always an outside chance of a Welsh cap. People were realistic, but after all, you never knew… and you could always hope for a game against one of the great international touring sides…

Yet for the last six seasons Penddawn, very much a second-class team, had swept all before them, unbeaten in all but a handful of games. We had, and were able to keep, an all-conquering pack together, led by the 'Mighty Morgans.' They were twin brothers who made a formidable second row indeed. This pack, my friends, were 'THE Terrible Eight'. Many are the myths of the Terrible Eight and many clubs claim that theirs was that pack, in some dim and distant past, but let me tell you, THE Fight were the Penddawn players of the 1930s!

It is said that after their last match they were put into a magic sleep by Rhondda's very own wizard and chemist, Willie Llewellyn, and it is said that when Welsh rugby is in need they will awake and lead Wales to glorious triumphs as in the days of yore. Then, to cap this great wealth of forwards, we had a kicker… Amyas Leigh.

Now, Amyas it must be said, was not the greatest full-back in Wales, in fact he wasn't the greatest full-back in Penddawn! But, by God he had a boot, a boot of prodigious skill. You must remember games were a lot slower 70 years ago; they tended to be dour forward battles with flashes of brilliant individual back play. Points scored with the boot while of course not unknown were by no means as common as today. Games may have been slower then but they were no less skilful, just different. And arguably, he said through clenched teeth, they were less entertaining than those matches of today; we didn't have squads, skills were individual, natural talent had yet to be coached out of naturally brilliant players. Much less seemed to happen in matches then, no less exciting, just played at a slower pace.

Matches were played for much of the season in great pools of mud, despite Dai's best efforts; scores of 3-0, 6-5 or 8-4 were common, double figures occurred of course, but not so often. Remember, a try was only 3 points, successful touchline conversions unusual, and long-range goal kicks practically unknown. I'd like to see one of today's 'Golden Boys' kick a 45-yard goal with a shapeless lump of sodden leather out of a great pool of water with no 6-inch tee to help him. When did you last see someone lying in mud holding the ball so a kick could be attempted? This was how Amyas earned his corn. An opposing team would give away a scrum, a simple 'knock-on', easily done, the pack would do their job, a quick kick to touch, and so on, then the forwards would grind away forcing penalties. With Amyas in your team any penalty within 40 yards of the posts was a chance. Also he could drop goals now. Despite being worth four points drop goals were a rarity; as slow as Amyas was, with that great pack in front of him he would often get given that vital second for a drop at goal. He'd miss some, but by golly he didn't half kick a few!

Formal representation had been made to the WRU for admission to the elite of the 'First Class'. However, 'It could not be,' we were told… 'there is no first class. All teams are equal… try and get some fixtures against other teams'… and we tried, and tried… There was as much snobbery among the committee rooms of those clubs and at the WRU as there ever was at Twickenham. A few offered to send their second teams to play us, but that was all. We were in no doubt they wouldn't play us for the simple reason of fear; they would not risk being beaten.

We'd made a desperate plea for a match against the 'Wallabies' who were due to tour in 1939, a futile request and we were told our pitch was 'not really suitable'.

Now at the start of the 1938 season things looked grim. A number of players had retired, and two, our second row, our stars, The Mighty Morgans had joined the exodus of those looking for work. No one blamed them, they were in love… and had gone to seek their fortunes, stalwarts, hard to replace at any time, but now we were the target for every team in South Wales… the fastest gun in the west was always there to be shot down.

The season started badly; matches normally easily won were lost. Dreams of glory, always faint, now all but disappeared. The 'I told you sos' from the other teams resounded.

'Flash in the pan…'

'Always very lucky…'

'Never really up to it you know…'

The WRU must have been feeling very pleased with themselves.

There was much debate about what could be done; there was not a little bitterness.

'Cometh the hour, cometh the man.' In our case it was RTD to the rescue… the die was firmly cast!

The first thing he did was get the Morgan brothers back from where they were labouring in Bristol, in his Rolls Royce of course. Such a trip is nothing today but, for us then, it was quite amazing. Gwyn and Mike returned on the Friday full of RTD's praises. 'Came to our digs, paid our bills gave us five bob each, a damn great pile of fish and chips and here we are, oh yes he's got us jobs as well.'

The very next day, in a real *Boys Own* style, they led the team to a crushing victory over our local rivals in what had been with the team's current form a much dreaded fixture.

The die was indeed cast…

Of course what RTD had done was totally illegal but, in those days of the totally amateur game that sort of thing went on, discreetly of course.

I suppose you could say the Penddawn team was sponsored by pub landlord Huw, not that the word 'sponsor' existed in that sense then. 'Patron' would be better. Anyway, all committee meetings were held in his pub, the team having no clubhouse. After every game he'd provide sandwiches, pies or a good old meal of faggots and peas, and there'd be a few jugs of beer. Good old Huw – he was a generous bloke. The team were fortunate in that they had a dedicated grounds man in Dai Clodge, who spent much of his spare time nursing the pitch like a mother her child! The golf players often moaned that he spent more time on the 'Parc' than on their greens and fairways. For his part, in his David Divot guise, he would simply say 'Priorities boys, priorities…'

Spectators stood on one of two grassy banks, beautiful in the spring and autumn, but a sod in the cold and wet. 'Yes, I had stand tickets… standing all bloody afternoon!' We also had a pretty good pavilion, no a damn good pavilion, which was shared with our soccer and cricket teams, a beautiful wooden building which wouldn't have looked out of place on an English green. No showers of course, two large communal baths – all good fun! Mind you not much fun when the rugby and football team were both home, with fifty guys sharing two baths being quite a sight! However, Huw had been a damn good friend to the team and he was quickly, completely and very cleverly replaced by RTD. Of course RTD realised he couldn't actually 'buy' the club... oh no, but he could certainly own it.

First off he bought the team a brand new strip. Fine, the old one was a bit past it to say the least, but the new kit was green... gone were the traditional brown and yellow hoops... 'I didn't think you'd mind boys... besides, green is lucky...' Let's face it, you don't look a gift horse... heaven knows the team needed a new set of jerseys... but we'd always played in hoops – we were the Giraffes. It was simply RTD stamping what little personality he had onto what he wanted, which was his own private team.

Very soon the pavilion had been completely refurbished. Owned by the council, mind you, and let's be honest, in need of some maintenance, yet somehow the soul was left behind under the coats of paint; but it was all paid for so thank you very much indeed. Can you guess what colour it was?

Also the great grass banks where we stood to watch the matches – they were concreted over and terraced, and let's be fair, that was an improvement, especially on a wet Saturday. Oh yes, things were looking up for the 'Greens'. Oh yes, The

Greens, decades of tradition wiped out overnight. Did it matter, or was moving that step closer to being a first class club so important?

Or was it too much, too soon?

Then came what RTD called his 'little Christmas present to the club'. Every man had a brand new blazer and a pair of greys. Remember, this was at a time when new clothes were a rarity; hand-me-downs were very much the order of the day; very smart the blazers, with just a hint of green, gone the old 'Giraffe' badge. 'That'll show those buggers in Cardiff.' Of course no one wore them to matches; they were to be kept 'for best'. And of course, THE COMMITTEE had their set to wear which they wore with a pride that would have made Joseph seem shy and retiring! The first new clothes I had that fitted were when I and many thousands went to do our National Service. Yes I had some new clothes ready for my start at Grammar school in September, money was available thanks to Dad's work, but although the money was supplied by Dad, the uniform was bought by the ever-economical Boppa… items were selected to 'allow room for growth'. Goliath could have fitted comfortably into my blazer, if he'd rolled the sleeves up. I was able to wear the trousers, my first 'longs' when I went for my college interview six years later.

RTD was a hero to many but, not all in Penddawn, but he was finally getting what he craved, namely RESPECT. The COMMITTEE then made a fatal mistake; it's just possible all would have gone well, but it was all going to turn sour. RTD had been made a life member soon after he brought the Morgan boys back to the team, then he became a vice president, then completely out of the blue the COMMITTEE created a special place for him and he was made a full COMMITTEE member with full voting rights... they always were a law unto themselves.

The team's successful run continued. Now as I've said, the pack were all-conquering, and the Mighty Morgans worth their weight in gold. There were some pretty magical backs too, but any team is only as strong as its weakest player and a team is what the 'Giraffes' were: a team. Perhaps a change or two could be made? But even the weakest of players was A Penddawn Rugby Man through and through, and all were staunch club men. This is what RTD did not understand... his belief was that every man had his price and the price those who may have been holding back his, yes *his* team must pay or they would have to go.

Quite simply RTD wanted to bring in players from other teams; outsiders.

Today transfers are everyday matters; money is involved,

contracts signed and so on; but then movement between teams was very rare indeed then. Money was not involved, at least not publicly; it just wasn't done. There was some movement between clubs; perhaps a young 'tyro' felt he was being kept out of his deserved place in the firsts, or an old stager would resent being dropped, or that old favourite – a complaint about being played out of position.

Perhaps a personality clash off the field would surface on the field and so on. So transfers, while not all that rare, did take place and there was usually a personal reason, or a slight, real or imagined, and all movement was within the small circle of Valley teams. And money never, but never changed hands – a pint, yes, but hard cash, no. But this was different. Players were brought in from outside… and it was soon fairly obvious that money was involved. Professional sport was all very well, boxing as we've seen was fine, and most clubs, both first and second class, had lost players to the paid world of Rugby League. These men were publically ostracised but often privately feted and spoken of with respect albeit grudgingly. The clubs, at least the second class ones, were secretly proud that one of 'theirs' had made it. And yes, RTD had given work to the Morgan boys, sort of acceptable but, strictly speaking, illegal… but now this…

It all kicked off when RTD somehow managed to

arrange a fixture with Neath. They were actually sending their first XV to play; it was to be a mid-week fixture, the last game of the season, and when the news was announced, well you can imagine how smug we all felt. We all basked in the reflected glory of 'OUR BOYS'. And no one basked more than RTD. There were still several matches to go but already the fixtures' secretary was sending out the letters for the next season… with RTD on his shoulder of course. Then at the COMMITTEE meeting just before the game against Parcglas – shock, horror – three members of the team were dropped; not through illness or injury; just dropped… they were not even replaced by players from the second team… there were three completely new names on the team sheet. Well, it was soon obvious what had taken place – RTD had persuaded or perhaps pressurised the COMMITTEE into accepting the changes. The players' representative on the COMMITTEE was Tom Morgan, now in work and happily married was hardly going to vote against his mentor was he? RTD's plan was to sacrifice established players with a policy of deliberately buying in outsiders whom he considered better players. The new men were all Valley boys known to us, good players all, but, not our players. Our team had, by and large, grown up together, worked together, sung together, drunk together… so the new players, individual skills apart and, fair

111

dos they were damn good men, however good they were, were not a part of 'OUR' team. The word 'LOYALTY' was heard… the newcomers' loyalty to their former clubs, abandoned in mid-season and Penddawn's loyalty to its players who had stuck with the club through thick and thin. RTD was heard to openly say, 'Loyalty? I can buy all the loyalty I want.'

Then word leaked out. RTD's plan was to form a Valley XV under the banner of Penddawn RFU consisting of players culled from surrounding teams… First class we might become… but at the cost of losing our team. That Saturday fixture saw one of the lowest attendances for a long time. It was too late, the die was indeed cast.

RTD had one more card to play…

Penddawn had no scoreboard, which wasn't unusual, as few teams did. Our cricket team were more sophisticated – they had a great board they'd 'found' at the colliery. It was painted black and gave all the relevant information: last man in, wicket standing etc., so very posh.

The rugby team, not to be outdone, made their own with timber again luckily 'found' on the colliery site. They built a great wooden table which wouldn't have looked out of place at Brobdingnag. Unfortunately, they got their sums wrong when they went to move it from the pavilion to its place of honour on the half way line… well put it this way, it took six men to get it into position! It was hastily fitted with wheels which didn't make it any lighter but it only took three men to move it!

We children loved it. It was our Hispaniola, our covered wagon, Robin Hood's oak and Nottingham Castle in one and after seeing *Beau Geste* it was Fort Zinderneuf! However… every sport has its scorekeeper be it rugby, cricket, darts or bowls – usually a former active participant who is glad to keep in touch with his sport, his friends and, of course, to help. The cricket boys had Ian 'Zin' Gary who sat quietly throughout the season on a rickety old chair keeping score meticulously.

We had Gareth 'Twenty' Williams… Twenty?… Well, he kept score, a score is twenty… 'Eye thenk ewe, and the next one right in here please.' Twenty had played for the 'Giraffes' as a young man, and a great future was prophesised, but he, like many others, marched away in August 1914, returning two years later sound in body but broken in mind. He managed, just, through the help of his butties, to keep working in the 'Co-op' but never played again. He took to RTD with open arms; he saw him as the club's saviour, 'He's the man to make us first class boys… he's the one to give us our rightful place…'

He took his self-imposed task very seriously; he would supervise the wheeling of the score table with a sense of ceremony normally accorded to the Ark of the Covenant. It would be placed with due reverence on the half way line. First he would cover the table with a vast sheet of oil cloth, on which he would place with great care his 'pay', two or three bottles of brown ale. Twenty would seat himself with great majesty upon a specially built a gargantuan stool from which hung a proportionately great galvanised steel bucket, and prepare for his duties.

These duties, it must be said, were not too arduous; fastened to the front of the table were two ordinary roof slates marked: 'HOME' and 'AWAY'; hanging from the front of these were a series of brass hooks on which Twenty would hang the scores; all very straightforward, all very simple. Unfortunately Twenty would have a pint or three before each match and this along with the brown ales caused two problems. He could not understand that when he looked at a number in his hand as a six, by what magic it became a nine when he hung it up. This along with his confusion over his left and right hands must be said caused not a little confusion.

It didn't really matter, as everyone knew the result and there was always a willing spectator happy to adjust the scores when Twenty's attention was elsewhere. The other problem would arise when a call of nature necessitated a break. He was too conscientious to leave his post; he took his job very seriously, and being unable to 'hang on' until half time or no side, I regret to say, the bucket would enter the picture... I'll leave the rest to your imagination... visitors were used to him, the oil cloth preserved his modesty. He was happy, offended nobody and hurt no one.

Then two weeks before the end of the season and the big Neath game, a horde of workmen descended on the Park. The men, all employed by RTD, set about laying a concrete base, and building a wooden structure not unlike a caravan. RTD supervised all stages of the building, and, with him, as proud as any peacock ever was, in club blazer and greys, was Twenty. RTD was recreating what he considered the ground needed, a scoreboard worthy of any seen by him in any American stadium. I must admit it looked damn good; it wasn't until many years later that I saw anything as impressive at any rugby ground. Of course it was nothing like any of today's monstrosities. Scores still had to be placed manually on hooks for instance, but in great green letters was emblazoned above it, very impressively: PENDDAWN RUGBY FOOTBALL CLUB... very nice it looked too. There was a place for the away team's name to be placed and already in position hung the name of our opponents of the morrow. But the *pièce de résistance*... it was electric! Mains electricity had been brought in from the pavilion; around the outside of the scorer's hatch, if you can picture it, were a series of coloured light bulbs, as

you see round a mirror in a theatre dressing room. And also…
a loudspeaker system… pretty crude by today's standards but
for us quite astonishing.

The Friday before THE game was an impromptu opening
ceremony, a dry run for the Saturday. RTD, all players,
COMMITTEE members and sundry hangers on were there
– blazers and greys were worn, of course, also similarly attired
was Twenty. RTD ascended the wooden steps to a scattering
of applause, switched on the lights, and very nice they looked.
The microphone was turned on and after a few shrieks,
whistles and 'one twos, one twos', RTD rattled off a few
meaningless words of thanks. He was keeping his proper
speech for the morrow. He hung up a score on the hooks –
Penddawn 36, Neath 3. 'I'll give them three; they might get a
penalty early on, before we get into our stride!' That was when
the trouble started. He'd been followed up the steps by Twenty
who now wanted to have his go on the mike… the speakers
relayed the brief sound of a scuffle and old Twenty was
promptly removed. RTD then made a mistake… the same so
many of us have made with a microphone in our hands… he
carried on talking… without switching it off. His words carried
as clear as a bell… pure Valley Welsh, no hint of American…
'Who let that bloody old fool in? Did the idiot really think I'd

let him loose in here? For pity's sake I gave him a blazer and greys. I want a bloody lock fitted on this door before tomorrow or he'll be getting in with his bucket.' There was a loud click as the system was killed. It was too late, most squirmed, looked at their feet, Twenty? He ran away, tears pouring down his face.

The Saturday was a beautiful day and the park was full by 2 o'clock, for kick-off at 3. The band was there, the male voice choir, and RTD turned up in his Rolls, with the mayor and a few councillors. All seemed set for a perfect afternoon, all unpleasantness put to one side for this, in all fairness, very special occasion for Penddawn. The teams took to the pitch early, for the speeches, and RTD and the mayor ascended the steps to the scoreboard, as RTD wished to address his admirers from high. 'Like Caesar!' was Eric's comment. 'Or Hitler,' added Larry.

However there was a problem. The door to the scoreboard… was locked! No, not locked, jammed from the inside. No amount of pulling, pushing or swearing would shift it. People quite enjoyed the sight; nothing like seeing a balloon of pomposity pricked is there. The Neath boys were highly amused! Finally force was applied… can you guess? Inside, crumpled on the floor was Twenty. He was wearing his blazer and greys… had three empty bottles of brown ale with him, and yes, his bucket… and yes, it had been used.

Dr. Manson was at the ground, an ambulance was called for, then cancelled, and he was gently carried away by his old mining butties performing their last rites for a fallen comrade.

The game went on; what does one do? There were no speeches or music, at 3 o'clock the ref blew his whistle and the game started. Unfortunately Neath hadn't read the script… their players fired up from the start were determined to put these upstarts firmly in their place. A second class team – RTD's imports – while talented, just didn't meld into the team; and to be fair, the Penddawn team didn't have their heart in it.

They were hammered… and with a fine sense of irony the score was 39-3.

We had a penalty early on before they got into their stride, and good thing they didn't have a kicker… only the score showed on Twenty's old table, hastily dragged down to play its part, as 93-3, to us. He'd have liked that.

The ground emptied quickly with only a smattering of applause. RTD was heard wailing, 'I gave him a blazer; I gave him the trousers, shirt, tie, everything… I gave him everything,' not realising that he'd taken away the one thing he loved.

Before the official inquest Twenty's mates held their own. He'd had a few beers in the Penddawn Arms, and left with his brown ale. It was still early and quite light. He'd gone to the scoreboard and bolted himself in, had his beers and fallen asleep. Waking in the dark, disoriented, he couldn't find a light switch, blundered around in panic, and just collapsed.

Death by natural causes.

SIGHT OF THE SEA

Meanwhile, on the bus, things quietened down as the initial excitement wore off, and for us children anyway, tiredness hit us, quite a few of us had had little or no sleep I can tell you. Some drivers knew the way. Some claimed to know the way and some alas, knew a 'short cut'. The bus was full of self-styled guides. 'I tell you last year we turned left at that junction.' They'd be put in their place by those who'd left the farms of their youth to seek their fortunes in the coal fields and were now on what was for them an annual pilgrimage through the land of the past.

Passing through St. Clears 'Old Bryn', now well into his eighties, recounted how his grandfather and father had told him how they'd gone out with their mates all dressed as women; the Rebecca Rioters, destroying the hated toll gates whose taxes seemed intent on taking the farmers scant profits.

One delightful moment; we'd stopped for what is now called a 'comfort stop', when the 'toast rack' came speeding past us, with all its passengers looking slightly windswept, pretending to be driving horses – a glorious moment! 'Mad bastards!' was one of the politer comments. 'Barmy Banister and those two mad buggers from the shop'. Though most agreed it was good to see them on the trip. I sat there listening, not being seen, while the two were being discussed. I'd only really heard Boppa's side of the story…

Eric, local boy, had gone to university some forty years previously, which was the equivalent for a valley boy of going to the moon. He'd come back to start his retirement and to care for his elderly father and to start the shop. His Conservative politics didn't make him too popular; he'd been one of the few men to favour Franco during the recent Spanish War. Although a number of locals did covertly support Franco, few had the courage to actually stand up and be counted. I'd heard it was only his age and health stopped him from actually going to fight in Spain. It must be mentioned that his support for Franco was a consequence of his absolute hatred for Stalin, and that gentleman's anti-Christian policies. His abhorrence of Hitler and his politics could not be doubted.

As for Larry; dear Larry. In his forties; Cornish, so 'not really English you know'. He'd been climbing in north Wales on the outbreak of The Great War, abandoned his university place, and joined The South Wales Borderers. The only Englishman in his squad, he'd been called, 'Taff'.

After the war he'd been touring Wales with a motor bike and a tent, visiting old comrades. The tent he used in wet weather to shelter his bike while he slept in the open.

He'd turned up in Penddawn, met Eric and the rest, as they say, is history.

I listened and learned.

It was a journey of, I suppose, some three or four hours to Pembrokeshire, to the 'Little England Beyond Wales'. The roads were not as good as today's roads, but there was very little traffic to hold us up, so it was a long old trip but a relaxing one. After the initial excitement, we all started to settle down, although some were still singing. Mainly it was just a general babble of noise, while a lot of us were content merely to stare out of the window at the new scenery.

Suddenly, an excited cry! 'The sea!… The sea!' And there was Tenby, perched on a hill overlooking the wonderful coastline of Carmarthen Bay. The buses parked at the top of the town and we formed a huge column and made our way down through the streets, with to me, their strange shops. We had money burning holes in pockets as we made our way through the town's curious narrow streets and past its mediaeval walls dripping with history. It was to be a few years before I would fully appreciate the history.

On we went, past the bustling picturesque harbour, down to its glorious beaches, its glorious, glorious beaches; then finally through the harbour on to the natural playground of North Beach, with its sand, rock pools and its terrifying, at least to me, then, Goscar Rock, a great monolith rising out of the sand. Funny how it became smaller as I got older. I always regret I never found the courage to climb it. I scrambled with my mates on the lower parts but never had the courage to make the journey to the top. I would always find an excuse not to go up… I was hungry, thirsty, or, my favourite, 'I can hear someone calling me!' Too late now, dammit.

Once established on the beach the two circle system was put into operation; a large inner circle drawn in the sand, in this inner sanctum, COMMITTEE MEN – families with no children – and let no child enter this circle! And then a vast outer circle, for families, and let no child leave this circle without an adult!

Of course, not everyone stayed on the beach; some wandered into the town to explore its delights, a few set off on the cliff top coast path to walk to Saundersfoot. Some went to South

Beach with its mile or so of sand and dunes and a view which included Caldey Island, while a brave few took the boat trip from the harbour to the island and its monastery where visitors could see the Cistercian farmers, and a fortunate few buy some of their perfume from the monks. The monks had no proper quay or harbour, but could be seen carrying their coal ashore on their backs through the waves from a 'delivery vessel'. We surmised fondly that hopefully they used Rhondda coal.

Nearly all of us children changed into our swim suits, and charged straight into the sea, of course that part of the sea covered by the rules of the 'outer circle'. There were no lifeguards of course, but plenty of grownups. Some of the men were clad in modern brief-type costumes, some in the older type which covered the chest. The ladies, well, some were in almost Victorian costumes; others a little more daring and rather fetching in one-piece suits. They came in with us, but most paddled contentedly in the shallows while we braved the depths, diving in and out of the waves. I didn't mind the water, it was heights gave me the willies.

Finally, back up to the beach to eat, with the crotch of your swimming costume around your knees – we called them 'bathers': a word considered by Boppa to be vulgar. These were usually home-made, or were almost certainly 'hand-me-downs', which deserve a chapter of their own! Made usually of wool (heavy as lead when wet, held up by a belt, both hands and a prayer) there were many green, blue and red bums if the dye ran; and they itched! And unfortunate was he who had to wear his sister's knickers...

An impromptu game of cricket was taking place; 'Catty and Doggy' had been banned seven years previously after an unfortunate accident laid out the local mayor who had come down in full regalia to greet the visitors to his town.

Meanwhile, a third circle had been drawn in the sand. A rough notice proclaimed that an alfresco/ad hoc/impromptu meeting of THE PENDDAWN LITERARY AND PHILOSOPHICAL SOCIETY was being held.

I edged over, and was quietly acknowledged by a few grunts, nods and winks; the members were indulging in the great game of TRANS-SIBERIAN EXPRESS.

I give you fair warning: this is addictive.

Eric's ambition was to travel on the Trans-Siberian Express. I wonder how someone as conservative as Eric would have managed with Stalin's regime. Of course, he may have fitted in very well! One would obviously need reading material for such a journey, some 4,000 odd yurts/versts/vests or miles or whatever. He'd ask us to nominate the ten books we'd take to pass the time on such a journey. It was THE forerunner of Mr Plomley's choice of records for a desert island. Nothing was easy where Eric was concerned; rules were hotly debated!

For example:

How were the complete works of Shakespeare counted? Some felt that they counted as one complete choice. That and nine other selections could be made.

Others supported the view that each play was one choice and one only.

But did this mean that *Henry V, Part I* was a choice, or were you allowed *Part II*, or was that a separate play?

Again, if the complete works of Shakespeare allowed, why not the complete works of Marlowe, or Dickens… and so on. There is, of course, no right or wrong.

I'm still playing the damn thing today, my choices ranging from *A Midsummer Night's Dream*, to *Three Men in a Boat*, via *Diary of a Nobody* to *Great Expectations*, with *Northern Lights* being the most recent addition, at the cost of *The Master and Margarita*, no, oh I'll have to keep that, it'll have to be *Lucky Jim*, wait a second… and so on… J. L. Carr, something by him, say *The Ragged -Trousered Philanthropists* MUST have that… and non-fiction… the list is endless…

Now, a little about 'trawling'.

Before setting forth on a trawl Eric and Larry would post a pack of leaflets to a friend in the area about to be targeted.

This friend, often an old college friend, would distribute the leaflets around the area, pushed through letterboxes in doors, placed in shop windows, and placed strategically of course in pubs. These would give details of what their requirements were – BOOKS! And where they'd be and at what time to discuss business; this meeting place was usually a café, pub, or even a friend's house. People would duly turn up and offer various items, and a deal was usually done. These leaflets were produced by a regular shop visitor, very rarely a customer, printer Aldine Bembo. Aldine lodged in a typical terrace with the ever tolerant Gill family. Tolerant doesn't describe them … he would have tried the patience of a saint!

For a start his printing press was a great old thing which filled a complete room. I don't think he ever paid his rent on time, if it was ever paid. The hours he kept were erratic to say the least; and to say he had an eye for the ladies is an understatement of understatements. However, his work was brilliant, some may even say beautiful, his wedding invitations were works of art, his posters for the local amateur dramatic groups were in the nature of *Latrec* himself. His biggest problem was his total unreliability. Wedding invitations would be ready a week after the week after the christening… Posters for amateur operatic productions would be delivered hours before the opening night. I still cherish the sight of the cast of the *Student Prince* in costume racing around the streets with posters, paste buckets and brushes hastily 'sticking' in between acts of the dress rehearsal. This included his good friend Richard Tudack, a keen thespian, who in full Prince regalia was racing down the High Street pasting furiously with Aldine scurrying behind him trying desperately to straighten his art work while crying, 'I thought it was next week… put them up straight… I thought it was next week… PLEASE put them up straight…' There were those who said it was better than the actual performance!

On one occasion a batch of trawling leaflets were ordered for a 'Trawl Fawr'. These were to be sent to several mid-Wales market towns such as Welshpool, Newtown, Brecon and so on. A trip like this, even accounting for the then excellent road and rail services, took a fair amount of planning. The leaflets had to be posted on and distributed; dates and times were crucial. Despite their pleading they were brought to the shop at literally the last minute; they were quickly checked, placed in envelopes and sent on their way with only a cursory glance. Alas, two of the towns' names and two the pubs' names had been confused…

So, in a place confusingly called 'Newpool', people were asked to bring their books to The Red Lion… but, the pub's name was actually The Black Lion. However there was a pub in 'Welshtown' called the Red Cow… This error, along with incorrect times and dates, led to not a little confusion for both sellers and buyers. This saw Eric and Larry scurrying between said locations with trawling bags, scattering hastily amended leaflets with a curse or several flowing from their lips… 'A bloody mad hatter's tea party organised by Charlie Chaplin,' was one of the milder descriptions.

However on this day at the seaside all had gone well. Leaflets had been produced well on time, carefully proof read and sent off.

Anyway, at about one o'clock, Eric said, 'Time to go.' So, gathering up our bags, we went. My first trawl had begun…

On our way into the town proper we looked across the sea at the romantic – romantic to me anyway – St. Catherine's Island, with its beautiful house. 'I could live there,' I said, my mind full of treasure and smugglers and Enid Blyton's 'Five'. 'Yes,' said Larry, 'I could live there, in solitude with the sea, my books and music.' He paused, 'Mind you, I'd build a bloody great steel bridge to the mainland first… and it would have a bloody great steel gate with one key!'

We strolled through Tenby calling into various shops and cafés and several private houses, asking if any books had been left. There were usually one, two, three or, even in one case a dozen. Money exchanged hands, and our bags began filling.

Eric passed me one beauty. I thought at first that with its distinctive orange and white cover and delightful logo it was a good old Penguin, but no, in this case it was a 'Puffin', adorned by said bird! It also had a small cartoon, of a scarecrow holding a baby! It was, of course, *Worzel Gummidge, The Scarecrow Of Scatterbrook*. It immediately appealed to me:a scarecrow that came to life! He passed me another, and this too had a strange title, 'You care for journeys, bach,' he said. 'Take this; it's about a journey to the edge of the wild! It's one of my favourites; I've an inkling you'll enjoy it too…' I didn't have time to look at either properly, because we were moving on.

We went next to a favoured port of call, if not itself a very popular place, to 'Uncle's'… yes, the Pawn Shop. While the two haggled with the owner I browsed his shelves piled high with the debris of people's lives when I saw a lovely egg cup. Now Boppa, bless her had very few pleasures in life, and one of them was a boiled egg! Today eggs are plentiful, but then, they were not as plentiful or affordable. A few of our friends had chickens and would pass on eggs, so some Sunday mornings saw us sitting down to a breakfast of boiled eggs, which were, I can assure you, a treat. We had a few chipped old china egg cups which did their job but this was a beauty. It's hard to describe; china, a sort of turquoise colour with a

131

sort of squiggle pattern, it just looked and felt – very hard to explain this – well, nice. Buying Boppa any sort of present was difficult. In fairness she wanted nothing, but whatever you gave her she was always so ungrateful. 'What did you waste your money on that for?… I've got one of those… take it back…' and so on. But she had let me come on the trip, and, in her own way, she was very kind to me. I'd take a chance. I took it to the counter where Eric and Larry were concluding their business, and from the tones, not very successfully.

I asked the price of the cup and was told 'Thruppence, now take it or leave it and clear off the three of you.' He accepted my coin and wrapped my purchase in a sheet of newspaper, and we left, I with a cosy sort of glow, the others, not so happy. 'Miserable old sod', and 'mean old bugger' were two of the most pleasant terms directed at the good gentleman.

However, we made our way to the 'Kardoma Café' where we were to meet up with Aldine, Richard and Sailor. Over a pot of tea, while I had pop, we examined our buys. I was just getting stuck into *Worzel* when Larry looked at my egg cup. 'Nice this Rod; porcelain.' That meant nothing to me. 'From Cornwall.' He continued. 'The Bernard Leach Pottery; big Japanese influence on his work. Who is it for?' he asked. All credit to him, when I told him his face remained totally impassive 'I'm sure she'll appreciate it,' he said.

132

Aldine and Richard then burst in, full of talk after their walk to Saundersfoot. Following hot on their heels was Sailor from the beach. He'd left his gramophone to continue the entertainment without him. 'Rod,' said Eric, 'here we must part. Go back to the beach with Aldine and Richard. We have to go to a final pick up, it's a pub so I'm afraid you can't accompany us.'

I left with Richard and Aldine and we made our way back to the beach where things were in full swing. The afternoon continued with its cycle of sea, sand, food, more songs, friendship, and another futile attempt on the bloody Goscar Rock. Finally, sometime after five o' clock, the job of packing up began. Some had already started to drift back to the transport, via shops and cafés. A group of volunteers were picking up the rubbish, as we weren't as litter conscious in those days, but the huge area we covered was left pretty clean; dammit, no, very clean. Mind you, there were a fair number of cigarette ends strewn about! Richard and Aldine gathered up all the bottles on behalf of Eric and Rod and put them in Sailor's pram. Glass was eagerly recycled, not that anyone had heard of recycling, but there was a penny back on each bottle and they had strict instructions from Huw to return them safely.

My mates and I hung about on the beach for as long as we could, squeezing the very last we could from the day; I think we knew it would be a long time before our next visit. As we wound our way tiredly back a tram clanged to a stop, Eric Larry and Sailor piled off, laden with bulging trawling bags. Sailor seemed as jolly as ever, but Eric and Larry had faces as long as time itself… 'Yes the pub visit had been successful; yes we met some old friends; yes we picked up a lot of books thank you.' But there was something wrong… And, on the walk back to the bus, Sailor filled me in on what had happened…. He also swore me to secrecy… so, having broken that promise once, I go back on my word some seventy years later, to recount the tale of the horse and trap, as Sailor told me through his tears of laughter…

A HORSE AND A TRAP

(A Cautionary Tale; A Sad Tale;
A Short, Pithy Tale With a Heart)

Now, it must be made clear, I was not there! But I feel as if I was. Dammit I SHOULD have been there. The tale is told as Sailor told me, plus various bits I gleaned from Eric later on. So this is the full, unexpurgated version, told for the first time, not counting my betrayal of trust that evening, of the events of the final stages of the Great Trawl of Tenby.

Larry, Eric and Sailor had made what was meant to be the final call of the day to an old friend of Larry's – yes, an old army friend. He directed them to a hostelry about a mile away which he told them usually had a few books behind the bar for customers. Of equal importance, he assured them it would be open – albeit illegally. Despite this attraction Larry and Sailor were ready to return to the beach and a good sit down.

Eric, however, swore it would be worth the effort. Who knew what treasures they might find – a great pile of books? The others advised caution. For once they had had sufficient funds to satisfy their needs for books and booze. Their trawl had taken them on foot and by tram several miles from Tenby proper. They were absolutely weighed down and it was getting late.

'We've had a good day; let's get back to the beach,' advised Larry. It was a hot day but the idea of a pint was obviously tempting… and at this stage I may add they were thirsty.

Eric was determined, 'We've got to at least look, after all we've got nothing to lose, and at the very least, we'll have a pint.' I don't have the name of the pub that was to be the scene where they met their nemesis…

Their thirst slaked they asked mine host if any of his customers might have some books they wanted to sell. The landlord just shook his head, for, as I was later told, 'Conversation was not his strong point.'

They were just drinking up when tragedy struck.

Eric's eye was caught by a crude, handwritten sign on a piece of cardboard, propped up against a bottle on the bar.

Grand Draw

1d a ticket

100 tickets only

Prize

A Horse and A Trap

'My good man!' exclaimed Eric, 'one hundred pennies for a horse AND a trap? It seems a little too good to be true.'

'I need the space. Draw is when tickets are sold, one hundred tickets, winner takes all…'

I'm told you could see the cogs of Eric's mind ticking over…

'So, if I was to present you with one hundred pennies – eight shillings and four pence, you would present me immediately with a horse and trap, both in good working order?'

'Yes', came the reply. 'Good offer,' he continued. 'Wouldn't do it, but I'm clearing out. Draw to take place when the hundredth ticket is sold.'

Now, you must remember, dear reader, it had been a long day, people were tired, not thinking clearly, and yes, drink had been taken.

On top of this, there was Eric's natural optimism and exuberance and, we must add to this, his eternal trust in the goodness of everyone. His eyes lit up, becoming bright with desire. He grabbed Larry, 'Think of it… the trawling… a trap, your tent, we can travel the valleys, Wales, the whole of the bloody country. Nights under the stars, the glow of the campfire, THE OPEN ROAD!' Eric was in full 'Mr Toad' mode (he may actually have gone, 'poop, poop'.)

'I tell you… I tell you…' He trailed away…

Larry was not, most definitely NOT interested.

'Eric, how the hell are we going to get the damn thing back to Penddawn? Where are we going to keep a horse? Who will look after it? What do you know about horses? They need a lot more care than just food – the cost of shoes alone!'

'Easy! Easy! Easy!' Eric roared.

'Barmy Banister of course!'

'We'll fetch him from the beach. You can drive the chara' back and me and Barmy will make our own way back. What can go wrong?'

Larry, the voice of reason was desperately trying to smother Eric's almost childlike exuberance.

He picked up the sign, and then fate played the card of destiny.

The cardboard, as I said, was propped up against a bottle, a liqueur bottle. Larry's eyes lit up as Eric's had. 'Green Chartreuse!' he cried. Now, to the good people of Penddawn, public houses sold beer, and they kept some spirits for birthdays, Christmas, high days and holidays, but, in the long run, it was good old beer.

Huw kept a special stock of rum for Sailor but beer was essentially the drink of choice not just for financial reasons, but by reason of choice, the pleasure of a bloody good pint.

Liqueur? Liqueur? What the hell was liqueur? Larry grabbed the bottle. 'Green Chartreuse, Green Chartreuse… my old friend.'

Larry, remember, had spent several years in France, as of course had many others, but they had generally stuck to beer, when available, or good old *vin blanc*. But Larry, somewhere along the line, had discovered and developed a love of Green Chartreuse.

Huw had tried – half-heartedly, it must be said – to get a bottle, but to no avail. Larry, as excited as if he'd seen The Promised Land, immediately called for three glasses! 'Nay, four! You'll join us, my good friend?'

This, addressed to the landlord, who knew a good thing when he saw it, soon caused four glasses to be lined up on the bar…

The deed was done.

The die was cast.

The scene was set.

The Rubicon crossed.

The drinks were poured; Larry then produced a box of matches. He smoked, as did pretty well all men, and while the others looked on in total amazement, he held up his glass and lit the contents. His companions looked on, somewhat puzzled to say the least, even Sailor, who'd literally been around the world and seen most things. Even he was somewhat taken aback.

Larry held the glass with its burning contents to the light for a second or two. 'Ahhh…'

Eric told me later that he had never seen him look so happy.

He blew out the flame and downed the contents, with tears of emotion in his eyes.

'Now you gentlemen,' he said as he lit their drinks and they followed suit – a lot more cautiously, apart from Sailor, of course, who swallowed his drink while it was still alight.

'Same again please!' cried Larry. They were getting into it now. As the four drinks burnt brightly on the bar, disaster struck!

Eric, reaching for his glass, knocked it over. A sheet of flame instantly spread over the immaculately polished and shining bar. In his desperate scramble to recover his drink he only succeeded in knocking over the other glasses!

They made brave attempts to slap out the flames with their hands, which only served to push the fiery fluid further and further along the now not-so-immaculate bar. The landlord desperately grabbed a bucket of beer slops from beneath one of the pumps and poured it on; this helped a little, but again, only succeeded in pushing the flames further. Sailor, was the man of the moment, he snatched a bar cloth and smothered the surviving flames into surrender. No one spoke for a moment or two.

Then apparently there followed volleys of curses, prayer and blasphemy which have no place here. After the initial outburst there were apologies – many heartfelt and profound.

There was only one thing to be done.

Eric spoke more low, but cheerily still. 'I pray thee then, this draw – can you assure us that there is no catch, no fiddle?'

'I assure you gentlemen, no catch, no fiddle.'

I'm sure now, for many of us, warning bells would have rung; any lingering doubts would leap to the surface. As I said, it had been a long day, the great bar fire had left us feeling indebted to the man, and reparation had to be made. Larry sat, head in hands, bewailing the imminent loss of either his money or his drink – it wasn't clear. Eric reached into the depths of a trawling bag and withdrew a brown leather pouch full of change. He emptied it onto the bar, and he and Sailor spent a minute selecting from the farthings, ha'pennies, thruppences and so on – one hundred pence – eight shillings and four pence, and, that was, I'm sorry to labour the point, that was a lot of money.

They passed the cash over.

Eric said, 'If you could keep our property here for an hour or two, I shall fetch our companion to prepare our prize and ready it for the journey home.'

'No need, gentlemen, no need. I shall fetch your prize and you may take it with you now.'

Oh dear.

Oh dear.

Oh dear.

As they sat, perplexed – still stunned – mine host re-appeared with:

A simple three-piece wooden clothes horse!

And…

(Can you guess?)

A mouse trap!

A trap indeed. I was told later there was no great row, arguments, protests…there was no point.

Their money was safe in the pocket of "mine host".

The deed was done.

As they stepped onto the tram which was to return them to

the beach, Eric philosphically remarked:

"It's all a matter of syntax, I suppose."

Well, that is the story that Sailor told meand is as good as place as anyto finish and resume our journey home.

THE END

Well, nearly the end, not quite, but bear with me, very nearly there.

The bus rattled up to the bunker and its cargo of happy, tired and fractious passengers began making their way home; not without a few tears and tantrums as the effects of the long day, and what seemed to be a much longer journey back, made its presence felt. Some of the children were playing up as well. I was still somehow as excited as I'd been some twelve hours earlier.

Waiting at the bunker were the Ellis twins; identical boys, Ross and Shaw. They had been unable to go on the trip as they were caring for their heavily pregnant sister, coerced by their redoubtable mother, her son-in-law couldn't stay with her, he was needed on the trip. A tenor voice such as his could not be left behind. Her husband had to go to keep an eye on him, and she had to go to keep an eye on him. OH yes he was on the COMMITTEE…

As well as keeping a general eye on the village à la Eric and Larry, the twins had therefore been delegated by the COMMITTEE, i.e. father, to see home any stragglers.

I jumped off the bus and ran excitedly, eager to spill my tales of the day, well, not that one; the road to hell is indeed paved with good intentions. I was being discreetly escorted by the Ellis boys, despite my protests of independence; it was only a hundred yards, dammit. The twins explained.

They spoke in half sentences almost telepathically, one or t'other starting or finishing the sentence.

'Sorry Rod…'

'Strict orders…'

'From your Boppa…'

'To get you home.'

'Safe and sound.'

Bursting with the thrill, the sheer excitement of my day, even the thought of Boppa's long face did nothing to curb my excitement. I expected to be sent straight to bed after having all traces of Tenby scrubbed thoroughly from me as soon as I stepped through the door, but this time it was different. I stepped in as she was sitting by the range, sewing basket out, darning socks, lost in thought. It was still light, hardly light enough to see, let alone sew, but plenty of time yet to light the gas. The Bible was there on the table beside her, open, ready for the Sabbath reading. But this time it was different. As I exploded through the door her face lit up. 'Here he is Miss Jones,' the twins spoke in tandem.

'Alive and well…'

'Been as good as gold all day…'

'No trouble at all…'

'Safe and sound…'

'As you asked…'

'He has behaved…'

'Perfectly.'

'How else do you expect my nephew to behave…?' Somewhat frostily…

'Oh dear,' I thought. 'Here we go.'

'However gentlemen, I am grateful for your kindness. He is obviously safer and sounder with you than others I could mention. Thank you both and goodnight.' They shuffled out mumbling in unison into the night.

As they left she threw her arms wide open. 'Come here, cariad and tell me all about it…'

Cariad…? Cariad…? She never called me that! I impulsively threw myself onto her lap and into her arms.

'Now, Rodney,' (Always Rodney, never Rod), 'tell me everything, don't leave out a single detail'… and so I told her everything… yes, EVERYTHING!

I started with the journey, the singing, the trek to the beach, the swimming; I delved into my now 'decent' trawling bag and strewed my shells and seaweed liberally mixed with sand onto the immaculate table and apart from a slight wince her face really seemed to light up… I gave her the newspaper-wrapped present. I waited for the usual tirade…? 'Why did you bother…? What a waste of good money…', but no!

'An egg cup! And what a beauty! Oh Rodney, Rodney, Rodney… you shouldn't have… Not to say I'm not grateful… oh bless you bach. You are far too kind to your old Boppa…'

And then, oh dear, I told her EVERYTHING! The full story of the 'Horse and Trap'. I know I shouldn't have, but, like Midas's barber I was exploding to tell… so I did…

And she laughed; she laughed and laughed and laughed… and I joined in until at last we were both sitting there helpless, tears drying on our faces. The fact of my betrayal hit me…

'Boppa, You won't tell anyone will you?'

'No of course not,' she said and I, quite rightly, believed her.

She then began to talk, and I for once listened, no, I mean really listened. 'That man called earlier this week.' I must have looked puzzled. 'That man… from the bookshop… when he called he spoke. He persuaded me, much against my better judgement I tell you, to allow you on the trip. He made it clear we must make the most of our time.'

'War,' he told me as if I didn't know, 'is going to start, sooner or later, whenever it comes it will be too soon but it was coming whether we liked it or not. It would be, he said, the last chance for you to have a trip, or holiday of any sort for a considerable time. Although I feel you endangered our home and did not deserve to go, least of all with those two...' She left her words hanging... I had to agree that my actions had been very foolhardy to say the least.

'Very soon, maybe this week, perhaps next week, perhaps not until next year, war will come. Mr Chamberlain, bless him, bought us valuable time. We now have conscription, our air force has had a chance to become stronger, and they will possibly be more important than the navy. Who knows? It will be in God's hands. However,' she continued, 'your friend,' she said with a sneer, 'has told me that things will be different after it has finished. For once, I agree. I don't know exactly how or even when but changes there will be; I think he may be right. WE, the working class won't be fobbed off with the Homes Fit for Heroes nonsense that was thrown at us after the Great War, the WAR TO END ALL WARS.... No, there will be changes. What exactly these changes will be, I don't know, no one does but we will have to adapt. First we have to survive the bombing, and of course... the gas attacks that must surely come... and of course after surviving all that, we must defeat Hitler...'

And, take my word for it, that from Boppa was quite a speech… and, I think you'll agree, somewhat prophetic.

Later, after we'd enjoyed a mug of sweet, milky tea and a slice of bread and marge and Boppa took me upstairs to my bedroom, the day really seemed to be over… then, glory, what a sight! My room had been transformed… No, not some great ridiculous TV makeover, but I saw two neat stacks of bricks with sawn planks atop for shelves, now wonderfully stacked with my favourite books taken from their box in the shop. A plain table, against the window, together with a kitchen chair, but on this table a wonderful thing indeed… an oil lamp.

Remember we had no electricity, downstairs we had a gas mantle in the kitchen, together with an oil lamp to light to save pennies, and of course when we had a power cut… yes even our meter ran dry at times. For the rest we made do with candles.

'Well,' she said, 'you're off to the big school next week; you need a place to do your homework, and to read I suppose, although you'll ruin your eyes.' I simply could not speak. Graham our next door neighbour had gone to Grammar School three years previously and he was forced to do his work in the outside lav with a candle. I not only had a room of my own, but the table faced the square giving me a room with a view. Glory, what a sight!

Let's put a few things into perspective: most, no nearly all of my contemporaries shared bedrooms with sundry brothers, cousins, lodgers and even sisters. Most shared beds, families were large and space was tight to say the least. I was one of the few who actually had a room of their own.

Boppa lit the lamp which filled the room with a beautiful beautiful golden glow. 'I'll fill the reservoir once a week and when that's gone, it's gone. Right, I'll leave the matches with you… I'll make no mention of the previous incident…'

I had, I hope, the grace to look ashamed, or at least try to look suitably contrite…

'Now ten minutes reading, no more… oh, you won't sleep tonight what with the excitement and the noise those layabouts will make later… you'll ruin your eyes, but there we are…'

My day, as my happiness was complete.

Taking my new book from my trawling bag I settled down contentedly into my chair, taking in the beautiful soft light given by the lamp… even now the faintest whiff of paraffin brings back that night. I don't know why we didn't call them 'paraffin' lamps!

I began to read 'In a hole in the ground there lived a …'

After the clock had chimed several times and after a warning shout from below, I reluctantly left my world of dwarves and dragons and riddles and runes. Finally cwtched into my bed, stone hot water bottle by feet, blanket round my ears, sleep wouldn't come of course as my mind raced round and round chasing the events of the day and the preceding days... thinking of elves, journeys, beaches... then the noise of another bus spluttering to the bunker drew me back to the window...

There was a chorus of shouts and cheers as a crowd poured out of the bus and exploded into the square and spread noisily through the streets to their respective homes or to the open door of the Penddawn Arms. It was like watching an old film where dozens of characters emerge from a single car.

The Ellis Twins were still on duty, 'to see home any over-exuberant revellers. And needed these were. Poor old Amyas Leigh had celebrated a little too well. Ross and Shaw gathered him up gently and took him carefully to number 33. Amyas, supported between them, burbled his love for them, mankind and of course his wife. She was waiting with a face which, even from my position, did not bode well for Amyas's future. She had obviously been nursing her wrath to keep it warm.

'Here he is Mrs Leigh.'

'Alive and well.'

'Been as good as gold all day.'

'No trouble at all.'

'Safe and sound.'

Alas, the familiar litany brought no thanks... She gathered her brows like a gathering storm.

'Oh! Oh! Oh! His glasses; his glasses,' she wailed. Indeed they were perched somewhat precariously on the end of his nose and did seem at risk. 'Take his glasses off.'

Duw, Duw, there's thoughtful I thought. Ross, or Shaw duly obliged and presented them to her.

'Here they are.'

'Nice and safe.'

'Like he is.'

'Both in the hands of loved ones... oh!'

As Ross, or Shaw finished Mrs Leigh welcomed her spouse, his glasses now safe, with a mighty right hook which Joe Louis himself would have envied; and would have undoubtedly been laid low had he received it. She'd obviously nursed her wrath and kept it very warm indeed. Ross and Shaw did the only sensible thing; they ran like hell back to the bunker to resume their duties, much shaken.

As I lay in that strange half-and-half stage between sleep and wakefulness I heard the last buses reach home and the revellers disperse. As the grandfather clock downstairs struck midnight I heard, through the mist of sleep and dreams, the unmistakable noise of the 'chara' arriving. And I swear I heard a great cry of 'WHOA MY BEAUTY!'

I peered through the window. Eric, Larry, Sailor and the pram wended their way through the streets, trawling bags groaning on their shoulders. Sailor had his precious gramophone on his head… and the pram… the pram was full of empties… The once full bottles of beer and pop had been lovingly gathered up by the trio to be returned to shop and pub for the deposits. 'Come on lads, leave the bottles here and have a beer with me.' Good old Huw. I think he realised that breakages were a strong possibility that late at night and he wanted to safeguard his stock. The Magi gratefully made their way into the sanctuary of Huw's Arms.

But wait, still it's not quite over… I fell into a deep and dreamless sleep only to be disturbed some hours later just as dawn was breaking. I don't know what disturbed me, well I do, I needed to pee, that late mug of tea… whatever, the Sabbath dawn was broken by a scream of:

'Bastards…'

'Swine…'

'Sods…'

I looked out of the window. A light from the pub showed things were still going strong in there, but, leaning against the bunker, in all his green-suited, hand-made Italian glory, his now somewhat dishevelled hand-made Italian glory, a cowboy boot in each hand, a man obviously in great pain and even greater distress… was RTD, Devious Davies himself… he'd been left behind.

Apparently at one 'refreshment' stop the bus marshal, a little under the weather, had been deposed of his position… and Llew had been appointed in his place. Now Llew had the gift, however much he'd had to drink, of appearing, stone cold sober. He'd of course taken his job seriously, clutching clipboard firmly, and conscientiously carrying out his imposed duty. However at the last stop, Hirwaun… he'd duly called the roll… and now starts the controversy… did he not call RTD's name… or did someone mischievously answer in his stead? Llew swore, 'I counted them all off, and I counted them all back on.'

It is one of life's little mysteries to which we have no answer but I know where my money lies. Remember, bus MARSHALLS never, but never, made mistakes…

The light in the pub vanished.

RTD stormed to the door, at least as well as a man with stockinged and sore feet can storm and began hammering against the door with both fists and a tirade of abuse that can be best imagined. Lights began going on through the streets.

An apparently bemused Huw shouted from an upstairs window, 'Go away you old drunk you, there's good Christian folk here trying to sleep.' If there is a God surely he would have been struck down.

The Ellis twins appeared from nowhere. (Well from the back of the pub actually).

'Come on now.'

'Oh dear.'

'How sad.'

'What a pity.'

'Never mind.'

'Mistakes happen.'

'Very sad I am.'

'I'm sure we all are.'

'There's a good man.'

'No need for all that noise.'

'And swearing.'

'On the Sabbath.'

They gently took him to his Rolls Royce. His chauffeur – duly collected by the boys from the pub – was in a somewhat distressed state, looking worse, if that was possible, than his employer.

He had not been allowed on his master's bus but had been obliged to travel on the "chara". Not that RTD was a snob, mind you, although some people did say he resented having his chauffeur in the same car as his good self.

RTD, no doubt sobered up by his walk, in a rage that can, I think, be imagined, rifled the wretched man's liveried pockets for the keys, threw him into the back, and, drove off, disappearing in the dawn. He was never seen in Penddawn again.

Sleep returned… it was over.

The day and my happiness were finally complete, complete.

I'm glad, so very, very glad I went on the Last Coal Trip To Tenby.

AN OUTBREAK OF WAR

Sunday, August 27th 1939

Well this was the last Sunday of peace, perhaps the last Sunday of peace of the last century, or is that a little too cynical, a little too profound?

Anyway, I sat at my window suitably scrubbed and suited, reading the passage to be learned for my reading in the afternoon. Passers-by could see me in my place of glory and some paused to wave, which I regally acknowledged. Their voices drifted up to me from the street… going to and fro… with the usual grown-up mistaken assumption that children who can be seen, can't hear every word. Tales about past trips which were a part of Penddawn lore… and new stories to be recalled in dark days to come.

'Better than last year…'

'Duw no…'

'What about 1927?'

'No '36, that was the one I tell you…'

And so, and on, and on…

New stories, lies and myths, call them what you will. The terrible tortoise stampede of Tenby… in 1936 or was it 37?

Already RTD's mishap had entered the canon of fact and fable, as had the great bar fire… and, I promise you, nothing else, until now that is. Forgive me lads….

Stories of couples who'd plighted their troth (in more ways than one) on Tenby's golden beaches, men who met women, women who'd met men. Marriages made in heaven… and of course the oft-heard cry of, 'Never again I tell you, never again!' Oh yes, Sunday dinner would be banged onto a great many tables this day I can tell you.

It was a long day; I was bursting to talk to my friends to discuss the day's events, but trapped indoors until the Monday, only allowed out on one of three trips, two to the Chapel, and one to Sunday School, where in a slightly more relaxed atmosphere we could exchange brief confidences.

You needed to be tough to survive A Welsh Sunday. The three hour sermon in the evening was something to be endured, I can tell you. There were no microphones and the minister's only audio aid was his voice. They did tend to rant and roar real fire-and-brimstone stuff, but the range of voice you would have to hear to believe. You'd be religiously sated, but, my word you'd be emotionally and physically strained and drained. Mind you the hymns were something else; the singing was always a real joy to enlighten the gloom.

Of course there were people such as Larry who had their own beliefs and those who had no beliefs who spent the day in their own ways, not that there was much to do, because everything was shut! Due to a quirk of the licensing laws the clubs were allowed to open. Well to be fair, the back door to the Penddawn Arms did tend to be ajar, which was where a number ended up. Larry refused to join any club as a point of principal as they were run by COMMITTEES!

Eric, after his Church service would make his way to the Conservative Club for his Sabbath libation. It took me many years before I stopped feeling guilty about my own, totally legal, Sunday drinking.

I'll never forget one Sunday a few years later. Da had just given me a camera as a birthday present. We had hardly stepped outside to try out the camera when Boppa's strident tones pulled us both back inside, for daring to risk the wrath of God by carrying out such an unholy action. Whether we feared God's possible future retribution more than Boppa's immediate fury is debatable! Sunday was a day of rest, but not a day of pleasure or enjoyment… God forbid. It says a lot

161

that after eighteen months in the navy and with a year's teaching under my belt my childhood training (fears?) were still deeply engrained.

It is easy to laugh and mock today but for many, many people it was what they truly believed and it gave them a very important 'light' during what was basically a bloody awful life with no light at the end of any tunnel.

Mind you similar thoughts probably ran through Mary Tudor's mind as she stoked up the flames. It took a world war to bring an improvement in lives, ironically a man-made holocaust making things better for many, but not all.

However, the next Sunday was to see, slowly at first, the start of many changes…

Sunday, September 3rd, 1939

'I'm speaking to you from the cabinet room at number 10…'

Well, you all knew it was coming, so let us get on. Hitler had invaded Poland, surprise, surprise… ultimatum issued… ignored… and so on…

That morning saw us, and millions like us, huddled around wireless sets and all doors were open for the many among us who had no sets. The vicar of St. Albans had taken his wireless to the church, available for all, regardless of denomination. A fine gesture, but… sorry Vicar, but we are chapel you understand. In our case we were at Mrs. Williams's house, Number 17. There were very few wireless sets in Penddawn and hers was the closest and her door was most definitely open, but, alas we could not go through it! To say she was house proud. I can't imagine in what circumstances she'd allow a known visitor into her house, let alone a stranger. When her husband had cut his throat in the kitchen she was really upset, 'Typical of him; he could have just as easily gone into the garden and saved the lino.' Rumour had it – totally unsubstantiated of course, but a story that had entered Penddawn folklore – that she'd made the ambulance men take their boots off before they could attend to poor old Ianto.

And poor old Ianto hadn't made a proper job of it either. After a short stay in hospital he was returned to an environment Howard Hughes would have found too obsessive.

On this momentous occasion the wireless was placed on a chair on a piece of immaculate lino covering the pristine area in front of her house. But we couldn't stand on the pavement, lino or no lino, heaven forbid. No, Boppa and I and about a dozen others stood silent in the gutter and road as Mr Chamberlain's monotonous voice confirmed what we'd all been waiting for. As we shuffled forward onto the gleaming white of her patch of pavement we'd be pushed back by a shrieking Mrs W wielding a mop. 'Get back! Get back!' So the earth-shattering news was lost amidst her cries and prods.

We all drifted home, gas masks firmly in place. The church and chapels were fuller than usual that day. Many indeed are the words that have been written describing life, and, of course, death over the next six years. For what they are worth, here are mine.

The first impact on our lives was the Blackout, and didn't we kids have some fun in that. And following hard on the heels of Mr Chamberlain's words, our evacuees arrived. It wasn't long before everyone had a 'vacuee story or two. The evacuees filled our houses; not for long in most cases. School opening was put back for a week but, as soon as it became obvious that the expected gas and bombs weren't going to devastate our cities, they drifted away, for a time at least.

For most of us our lives didn't change at first. It was several months before the mines started to re-open, and quite some time before coal production was in full swing. Larry went back to his beloved regiment. He apologised to me, 'As a Buddhist I suppose I shouldn't go off to be a soldier, but this man needs to be stopped; then after him… probably Stalin.'

Sailor went back to his beloved ships, catching his train to Plymouth, 'First time I've used public transport in twenty years.' His trolley was left in the yard of the shop and his gramophone in the shop where it continued to be the source of music for customers.

The Americans called it the 'Phoney War'. Not very 'phoney' if you were Polish, and not very 'phoney' for Mr. and Mrs Stevens, one of whose sons died when *H.M.S. Courageous* was sunk, and the other when the *Royal Oak* was torpedoed in the 'safety' of Scapa Flow… oh, yes, very phoney from the safety of 3,000 odd miles.

In fairness, for us at least, things weren't too bad, and apart from the Blackout life wasn't all that different for a while. It was after several months and the bitter winter of

1940 that I suppose things began to change. Mines began to re-open… and then in the summer things really took off. Many are the books you can read about this period; the German armies smashed through Europe, there was the fall of France, Dunkirk, Churchill came to power, and what power, and we stood alone, well 'aloneish'. Australia, New Zealand and India and many others stood with us.

While The Battle of Britain raged we children went on much as before, our play interrupted by collecting 'scrap for Spitfires', while the men joined the Local Defence Volunteers, later called The Home Guard, of course now known and immortalised as 'Dad's Army'. Eric duly enlisted in their ranks and was sent home after one evening. He'd turned up with his carving knife duly attached to a broom handle as instructed and after one brief period of weapon training was told that by enlisting in the German army he would be our greatest asset!

Then came the Blitz, the assault on our cities and towns from the air, and the return of our 'vacuees. In Penddawn our sirens would wail their warnings as the aircraft made their way to Cardiff, Swansea or even our beloved Tenby; and while a few had proper shelters most of us took refuge in the cwtch under the stairs.

Generally the war passed us by, employment was at an

all-time high. Food rationing generally improved people's diets. We clung to our newspapers and wireless sets; eager for news… Africa… Singapore… Hong Kong… Pearl Harbor: The Yanks came, lots and lots of them!

And life carried on.

That night was the same as many others; we were dragged by the sirens from our beds into the cwtch. At this stage most of us had given up sheltering, preferring to remain in bed. Boppa, however, insisted when the sirens went we must take cover. Usually we would sit in silence; yes a companionable silence. I would try to read by candlelight, while Boppa would knit. We would occasionally hear the faint drone of aircraft, or imagine we could hear them. This night, as we sat quietly, something caused us both to look up. Then, one almighty explosion… the whole house shook, a great cloud of dust came down, then silence. 'Goodness,' said Boppa, 'that was close; Cardiff I shouldn't wonder…'

Bless you Boppa… an enemy aircraft passing overhead possibly attacked by one of our fighters, released its load, a landmine. Basically it was a bomb, a bloody big one, attached to a parachute, designed to drift silently down and land without penetrating the ground so its explosion would spread unabsorbed to cause maximum damage.

As it drifted down P.C. Copper, (yes, Copper the Copper) saw it and ran towards it assuming it to be a parachutist...

The bunker took a lot of the blast. The solid concrete block was completely flattened but it served us to the end and absorbed much of the explosion... a lot... but not all...

Six houses were flattened in River Street, a dozen or more fronts and or roofs blown off... windows shattered... dust and debris... the smell...

Men and women poured from their homes, survivors clambered from the debris, shattered physically and mentally. The women brought with them a lifetime of dealing with traumatic death and responded as they knew best with blankets, tea and sympathy. The men grabbed what tools were available, and many with their bare hands, using their lifetime skills, began burrowing into the smoking debris. They brought out fifteen dead adults, twenty injured... and six evacuees, as safe as... well houses. They were brought out into the arms of the waiting women.

While the grown-ups had stayed snug and secure in their beds, those with first-hand experience of the havoc bombs could cause had fled to safety under the stairs at the first wail of the siren; Boppa was there, one of the many assisting, and I – despite strict instructions to the contrary – was watching with my mates.

There were no flames, furniture and carpets were piled in the streets, the fire brigade had damped down the smoking debris, which gave off a damp and evil stench adding its own taste to the atmosphere of death. Even now the aroma of bonfire can transport me back.

Eric, who had been helping, i.e. keeping out of the way, stepped in. He gathered up the children whose homes from home were smoking ruins (their Welsh 'aunties' and 'uncles' dead or injured) and took them to the shop. As he ushered them away he turned and briefly waved, 'Go home, Rod bach, nothing to see.' I never saw him again...

Two hours later, a solitary plane, probably lost, who knows, probably some scared Germans wanting nothing more than a swift return to the Fatherland, dropped its bombs, causing more explosions crashing through the night and as a result numbers 81, 82, 83, 84, 85 and 86, Heol y Groes ceased to exist. There were further rescues, more cups of tea... but there was no rescue for Eric or the evacuees...

His living room, through a quirk of the explosion, remained intact... he sat in his chair, the Puffin copy of *Worzel Gummidge* in his lap, the children sitting and lying on the floor, listening with rapt attention to a wonderful story read by an expert for eternity. Then, all dead... no marks... killed by the blast... taken from their homes to a safe place and so it goes....

The next day life in the Valley carried on normally, for most anyway. We'd lived daily with death; it was as people said, 'A part of life'. This was no different; it was personal, but you had to carry on, 'You can't let the Hun show he's on top.' 'Stiff upper lip. 'Britain can take it', and so on.

I couldn't take it. I lay in and on my bed for hours staring at the ceiling; an ache in my belly that would not go away, despite the endless cups of strong, and, despite a sugar shortage, sweet tea. Bless you Boppa.

I finally shook off my torpor and made my way to the scene of the previous night's destruction. The buildings had been roped off, the debris was neatly piled; glass had been cleared away, slates, timber and all recoverable materials were stacked, they'd be needed for repair work. Furniture was piled on the road; it would be there for those still alive, those who had nothing. Eric's room stood intact, proud among the ruins. As I watched, the recovery men were getting ready to pull it down.

The books from his room had been placed in boxes. Those from the shop were strewn across the road, some intact, some shredded in a mad scattering of confetti. Others were welded by the explosion and water into thick-packed compact blocks as solid as the bricks that had once supported them. All smelt evilly of smoke, dust and somehow misery, and even, dare I say it, of death.

I just stood and stared, unable to take it in. War happened in other places, not in my home, not to my friends. I gave voice to my feelings. 'It's not fair; it's not bloody fair…'

'You are quite right Laddie, it's not fair, and in fact, it's a right bugger.' It was Larry, sent for by telegram. He pulled a chair from the stack and sat me on it. 'Wait there cariad.' He poked among the debris, and sorted through the once friendly boxes, ignoring the warning calls from the site workers.

He came out with – a fine irony this – the wooden explosives box which had once been such a source of comfort to me, and held so many 'friends' of mine. 'Here, take this Rod.' It now held Eric's copy of *A Christmas Carol*, the Puffin copy of *The Adventures of Worzel Gummidge*, which I'd not seen since that day in Tenby, two old enamel mugs, and the till, an old box which once held bottles of hair oil. Remember? And, it smelt too, not of that night's destruction, but rather as if it had absorbed everything that was good in the shop. Can inanimate objects hold feelings? These could; they gave off warmth, love and friendship. They smelt of Eric.

Larry walked back with me to Boppa's, where she gave Larry as good a welcome as she could. He stayed with us for several days and we grieved together.

171

Well, we got over it, you've got to. Public grief, private mourning. I had only just left Junior School, at that age nothing really lasts. I was eleven and going to live forever.

The funerals were spread over several days, services were held in our chapels, and prayers said throughout the valley. The evacuees were buried together in Parc cemetery. Eric's funeral was held in the church; the vicar, a close friend of Eric's, asked Larry to read a lesson. He politely refused, and suggested me. I sat for hours looking for a suitable passage. Finally Boppa took up the Bible and said, 'Here, this is the piece you want, Proverbs, very suitable. No. Don't read it now; keep it for tomorrow; read it fresh. It's what he would have wanted…' Now, where had I heard that before.

Next day I stood proud in the pulpit, totally in awe of the trappings of the church and shaking like a leaf as I turned to the open Bible and read, my voice strong and proud, 'Proverbs, also known as The Song of Solomon, chapter two, verse five'… I looked at the text… Boppa had chosen this?

'Stay me with flagons, comfort me with apples: for I am sick of love…'

How I managed to get to… 'His left hand is under my head…' Somehow I kept going, and as I returned to my seat I saw the shaking shoulders and heard the muffled chortles from the members of the late Penddawn Philosophical and

Literary Society… 'Well done,' said Boppa, wiping a tear from her eye… of sorrow or mirth? Was the unfunniest person in Wales capable of such a thing? 'Well done, cariad, exactly what he would have wanted.' We took his coffin to the churchyard for the burial where Larry and the Dark Lady waited, together. After the vicar had finished his words Larry read, parts of the beautiful and moving *Cynddylan's Hall*, which starts…

Stafell Gyndylan ys tywyll heno,
Heb dân, heb wely.
Wylaf wers; tawaf wedy.

The poem wasn't fully understood or appreciated by some of those there; but, those who did, shed not a few tears. Eric, and the others who'd perished, all left legacies, not physical bequests, but memories in our in our minds, minds made so much better by their own.

The grown-ups either drifted to their homes or adjourned to the Penddawn Arms for drinks. For want of anything else to do I walked the two miles and went to school. I'd done my crying.

Larry said his goodbyes to us that evening. The books he'd manage to salvage he took to the Miners' Institute. 'Remember

Rod. Never read a sequel, and never ever see a film of a book you've enjoyed.' Pretty good advice. And as he left he called out 'Oh yes, don't forget, "Travel light my friend, travel light."'

He returned to Penddawn several times over the next few years, never failing to visit us. As soon as the war finished he left for India… 'Searching for Nirvana Rod…' I do hope he found it.

And that, I suppose, is it.

Life carried on; it always does.

The war in Europe ended. We had a huge street party which culminated in a huge blackout-free bonfire, and oh yes, it saw the cremation of RTD's bloody scoreboard, not, I hasten to add, 'Scorer's' magnificent table, which survived and gave service for many a long year.

Bombs were dropped in the East.

Da came home for good and the "Co-op" closed for good.

I matriculated, worked in a solicitor's office which I hated; embraced National Service; eighteen months in the Royal Navy, a 'bunting tosser' on minesweepers, which I loved.

Two years teacher training, then thirty years at the 'chalk face' of History and English in Penddawn 'Sec Mod'. Later a 'comp'. Heaven alone knows what it's called today.

Life changed, slowly, steadily, as 'progress' made its inevitable way.

The influence of the chapels has dwindled, as has that of the church. Apparently in 1906 there was one chapel for every one hundred people in Wales, although it seemed a damn sight more to me. Now they are closing at a rate of one a week, becoming Boys' Clubs, carpet shops, curry houses, nurseries, and homes. One has been taken down and re-built in Japan as a golf club... what the good Parchedig Evans would make have of I'm not sure. At least they are in use as, so many are left derelict; better knocked down than left crumbling relics of a bygone age. The way the oldest chapel in the Rhondda was treated, or rather the way it wasn't treated, was appalling. I don't know if one has been made into a second-hand bookshop or not... now there's an idea....

And the mines... yes the mines... all gone. This is not the time to get me into a rant about that; no place here to relate the story of strikes and Mrs. Thatcher. One Welsh mine is now a museum which has visitors from all over the world experiencing the underground experience. I heard one old collier say, 'I spent all my life going down a bloody hole in the ground praying to return to the surface... and now people are paying to go down a bloody hole in the ground!' More and more houses were modernised, the old ranges ripped out, coal ceased to be the source of fuel, being replaced by electricity and gas. Front rooms began to be used for families to actually sit in and enjoy themselves, not just for best.

Mind you, these changes didn't happen overnight and for many they didn't happen at all. And a large number of these 'fully modernised homes' still had the lav, 'out the back'.

The coal trips finished, and of course, the bunker had ceased to exist that dark night. Seaside trips continued, money was plentiful; excursions were organised by the Labour, Con, Liberal, Hibs and Caledonian clubs; even the chapels ran their own trips. They went to all the old favourites: Porthcawl, Barry Island, Aberavon and of course my beloved Tenby... but it was never, for me at least, the same. Yes, the same people, the same anticipation, even largely the same trip, but it was different. Times were changing; Billy Butlin had even built one of his camps at Barry Island.

People began taking holidays for days at a time, there's posh! Staying at bed and breakfasts, guest houses, or even, heaven forbid, hotels. Now that was posh. Camping and caravans were popular, and soon flights to Spain... and the organised trips began to dwindle, although they continued well into the '70s and '80s. Porthcawl boasted the BIGGEST CARAVAN SITE IN EUROPE!!! And many, many went there, many times. One street goes there en masse for their annual holiday, showing that the spirit of the coal trip still exists and is as strong as ever. But now even the pubs are closing. The Penddawn Arms, run by the same family for nearly a century, is now an empty shell. Landlords (and landladies) came and went with a frightening speed. Many other businesses in the same family's hands for generations have closed for ever. Those beautiful ugly slag heaps have gone and the Valley is green again... yes the Valley has changed, but the people are the same. 'Community' with a capital 'C' indeed.

And as for me... after a failed marriage (my fault) and a chance meeting with an old college friend I made the move to Cornwall. I took very little furniture. Bookshelves and books filled the removal van and fill my home. Here I live within sound, sight and taste of the sea. Nearby is the pottery where Boppa's egg cup was made and which still graces my breakfast table. The 'till' survives on my mantelpiece; I use it for loose change. And I still light a candle every March 8th and remember good times.

I left many good friends when I moved, but new faces have filled gaps. My oldest 'friends', books, are cheaper today and much more readily available; I can't move for the damned things! I still indulge myself by playing 'Trans-Siberian Express.'

It is a good place to live; much in common in many ways with my valley home. I suppose it is very similar, a great industrial area laid low in the 21st century. I suppose you could call it Penddawn with beaches! And the people, there is no real difference there; they are very much the same.

Once a week I walk out to the 'Island' where I keep a lookout over the waters of the Bay with my fellow volunteers of the National Coastwatch Institution. We provide a service which Her Majesty's Government saw fit to remove. Our station houses radar, a computer, GPS and all sorts of electronic wizardry. Even so, in this day of satellites our station and over forty others provide an 'eyes-along-the coast' service which no amount of technology can replace. You still can't beat the 'Mark One Eye Ball!'

I received my training from local stalwarts: Bill, Malcolm and Terry, and of course 'Trevor the Treasurer', who, between them, and with the patience of saints, made this lifelong technophobe into a watchkeeper. It's a worthwhile way to spend your time and lets me put something back into the community in which I live. When I'm at the lookout station I can remember good times in the navy and yes, great times at the seaside.

My local library has a friends' group who meet and invite guest speakers, writers and the like to talk about their lives. These speakers play their version of 'Trans-Siberian Express', but they list their 'Desert Island Books'. I find myself agreeing and disagreeing with their selections and changing my list constantly; these evenings send me back 70 years to argument and discussion in shop and on beach about what we would have taken... *Three Men in a Boat, Worzel Gummidge, The Ragged-Trousered Philanthropists*. So many books, so little time...

Oh I'm glad, so very, very glad I went on The Last Coal Trip to Tenby.